SCARLET FEVER
Hill Country Heart 2

Sable Hunter

Sable Hunter

This is a work of fiction. Names, characters, places and incidents are either the product of the author's imagination or used fictitiously, and any resemblance to actual persons, living or dead, business establishments, events or locales is entirely coincidental.

Scarlet Fever
All rights reserved.
Copyright 2012 © Sable Hunter

Cover by JRA Stevens

ALL RIGHTS RESERVED. This book contains material protected under International and Federal Copyright Laws and Treaties. Any unauthorized reprint or use of this material is prohibited. No part of this book may be reproduced or transmitted in any form or by any means, electronic or mechanical, including photocopying, recording, or by any information storage and retrieval system without express written permission from the author / publisher

Alex Stewart has been roped into playing wedding co-ordinator for his older brother Ethan's wedding; and nothing is going right. To make matters worse, he gets off on the wrong foot with the bride's delectable sister. Before he knows it, Alex is suffering from a raging case of Scarlet Fever, and is determined to claim this woman for his very own, even if it means making a sacrifice he never thought he would make.

Scarlet is taking a trip to see her sister get married, and to experience a small taste of a normal life. After setting eyes on her too-gorgeous soon-to-be brother-in-law, Scarlet decides Alex is way out of her league, and strikes off #1 from her bucket list - losing her virginity to someone she trusts. When Alex finds her list, and discovers the secret she is hiding from everyone, he is determined to help her anyway he can. Can he break through her stubborn pride and make her see she deserves a life? Preferably with him!

Content Warning: Contains adult language and sexual situation. Not intended for young audiences. 18+ only

CHAPTER ONE

Scarlet Rose Evans had a bucket list, "100 Things I Want To Do Before I Die". She sat up in her bed, her bottom cushioned on a thick pillow, notepad on her lap, and crossed off two items on her list. Number fifty-seven had been a disappointment, *War and Peace* was depressing, and she didn't want to waste any time being depressed. Number fourteen, however, had made her smile, even if it had made her bottom sore. Scarlet had giggled while trying to hold a hand-mirror at just the right angle so she could see the small, scarlet-red rose that now graced the top of her left hip.

If the Board of Deacons had any inkling that the Church Administrator of Pine Forest's Lutheran congregation now sported a tattoo on her butt, she would probably be churched, the Lutheran equivalent to excommunication. Looking at the bright spot on her bottom, Scarlet decided it was worth it.

Climbing from the bed, she laid her list down, and pulled off her white eyelet gown. Without a single glance in the mirror, she walked naked to the shower and turned on the water. Scarlet had trained herself not to look in the mirror. She hated to be reminded of what other people saw when they looked at her.

Allowing time for the temperature to get bearable, she brushed her teeth. Today was going to be exciting, she was about to pack up and travel to an enchanting Bed and Breakfast, *The Lost Maples*, and help her beautiful sister get ready to marry the only man she had ever loved.

After a great deal of planning, Scarlet had been able to take two weeks off from both of her full-time jobs. At present, she divided her days between the small town library and the offices of the local Lutheran church.

Luckily, the two esteemed institutions were built side by side on the main street in town, and she could run—or her version of running—from one to the other as was necessary.

In addition to her 'eight to five' commitments at the church and the library, Scarlet kept herself busy in a half a dozen different ways. One of her favorite things was making cookie mix in a jar. She would take a mason jar and layer it with all of the dry ingredients necessary to make a batch of cookies. Topping it with a piece of gingham and a ribbon and she had a cute gift to sell. Remembering how much Annalise missed her cooking, she slipped two of each kind in a bag to take with her on the trip. She also made hair clips from tooled leather and various silver charms and gemstones.

Scarlet did anything she could to make a little extra money. Her favorite extracurricular activity was sewing. Homemade clothes weren't exactly in vogue, but Scarlet had a gift, some said. Her customers said the work she did looked as good as the best custom tailoring. Her specialty was making wedding gowns for brides who longed for a beautiful dress, but just couldn't afford the high prices the designer boutiques charged. The dress she was fashioning now was the most important one she would ever make. Scarlet was sewing her sister, Annalise's bridal gown. Years ago, Annalise had torn a photo of her dream dress out of a popular bridal magazine. Now, Scarlet was doing her best to recreate it. The only phase that was left to go was the final fitting, and then the sewing on of countless seed pearls. The blinding job of sewing on the tiny pearls could be done after she arrived at *The Lost Maples*. Nights were long, and it was always better to have something to do with her hands. If she kept busy, she didn't spend so much time thinking about her future and how short it might be.

Other than sewing, she took in ironing—another lost art—and she baked wedding cakes. It took every dime that she could manage to rake and scrape together to buy the medicine that kept her alive.

Standing in the shower, she soaped herself, fantasizing what it would be like to feel a man's hands on her body. It was an experience that she had not, as of yet, been fortunate enough to experience. She did dream about it, however. Often. Fantasy men weren't hard to please. Scarlet was very afraid that her body would not be enticing enough to satisfy a real flesh and blood man.

Running her own hands over her slightly heated flesh, she took inventory of her meager assets. Her waist was small and her hips were all right, she supposed. Glancing back at the tiny rose, she imagined a man tracing the small tattoo with his tongue. The thought made her shiver. Sadly, she was woefully lacking in the breast department. Scarlet cupped her own breasts, imagining what a man would think of their less than generous size. She shivered, not with delight, but with dread. This unfortunate flaw in her body was going to make the first item on Scarlet's bucket list more difficult to achieve. Her best hope was still Alex.

Alex Stewart was her sister's future brother-in-law. And to hear Annalise tell it, he was a knight in shining armor, Prince Charming, and Casanova all rolled up into one super good-looking guy. Scarlet didn't doubt that her sister loved her fiancé Ethan with all of her heart, but Ethan's brother, Alex, had been Annalise's rock. He had encouraged and counseled both Scarlet's sister and his brother through their bouts of doubt and hopelessness. Annalise thought Alex hung the moon. And Scarlet needed someone like that—a hero—just for one night.

Stepping out of the shower and drying off, Scarlet dressed quickly in blue jeans and a pink lace camisole.

She didn't bother with a bra, she didn't need one. For a while, she had worn a padded bra, but had determined that was sort of like false advertising.

Picking up her bucket list, she circled the number one item. It read, 'Make Love'. She knew there was no one in her small home town that she could ask to do this for her. In the eyes of all the men that she had grown up with, or knew around town, she was still the awkward, sickly girl with the malformed foot. It really didn't matter that the good people at the Shriner's Children's Hospital had fixed her misshapen club foot seven years earlier. Beauty will always be in the eye of the beholder, and the men of Pine Forest would never see her as anything other than a deformed cripple. Scarlet could walk fine, now, except for a slight limp. One leg was still about an inch shorter than the other. Most days she could keep her gait even enough that it wasn't very noticeable. But when she was tired, there was no way she could hide it.

In her quest to have her one and only experience with sex, Scarlet was actually considering trying to contact a male escort service while she was in the Austin area. Sunday nights had brought a television show into her living room that featured a really nice guy as a gigolo, and if she could have been certain that she would be hiring a guy like him to take her virginity, it might be all right. There were no guarantees in life, Scarlet was smart enough to know that. Paying someone to have sex with her would be a last resort. In fact, the idea of giving herself to an uncaring stranger made her want to cry. Losing her virginity was a milestone that Scarlet would hate to miss, so she wasn't ruling anything out, but she was determined to see how it went with Alex first.

Blowing out a frustrated breath, she looked at her pale face in the mirror and admitted the sad truth. Knowing herself as well as she did, when push came to shove, she probably wouldn't have the courage to actually ask someone to make love to her—either for money or as a pity f**k. Ugh, she was so innocent, she couldn't even think the word without the asterisks or blushing. Unfortunately, time was definitely a factor.

If all went according to plan with Alex, she could experience love-making—just once—while she still felt half-way decent. As luck would have it, Scarlet had been allergic to the anesthesia administered to her during her foot surgery. Her kidneys had suffered irreparable damage. The verdict was hard for her to face, but the doctors had informed her that she had, at most, one more year before she would have to have a transplant. With no way to get health insurance, and being as poor as the proverbial church mouse, the likelihood of a transplant was just about nil. Sadly she smiled to herself—church mouse, that's what the men of Pine Forest called her, behind her back, of course. People could be cruel.

So her bucket list was important. Scarlet wanted to experience all that life had to offer, and she was running out of time.

When she got to the B&B and met Alex, she would know whether or not she had the courage to try and seduce him. The thought made her laugh. She couldn't picture herself seducing anybody. Still, when you knew this might be your only chance…

* * * *

Ten days before the wedding…

The *Lost Maples Bed and Breakfast* was located in Vanderpool, Texas, very near to the State Park of the same name. The park was home to the out-of-time, out-of-place stand of Bigtooth Maples that was so highly unusual this far south of the Mason-Dixon Line. Scarlet was so excited. Seeing the brilliant reds, burgundies and golds of the maple leaves without having to travel to the East Coast was such an opportunity, and also number thirty-two on her list. Travel items on her bucket list were few and far between. Traveling cost money, and that was one thing in short supply at Scarlet's house.

Placing an Elvis CD into the player, she began to sing in a loud, clear voice. Singing was one of her joys. She had performed at local functions for years, weddings, church meetings, fraternal celebrations—any number of places. One woman had asked her years ago where she had received voice training and she had answered truthfully, 'in front of a mirror, singing into the end of a candleholder, providing back-up for the King of Rock and Roll'. Scarlet loved Elvis. Going to Graceland was number two on her list. Chances were slim to none that she would ever get to go, but she liked to keep it as a possibility. It *could* happen.

It was a six hour drive between Pine Forest, which was on the Louisiana border, to the Hill Country of Texas. According to her agenda, she planned to spend the first week of her vacation with the wedding preparations and—maybe one romantic interlude with Ethan's younger brother. 'Romantic' wasn't *exactly* the best word, but she refused to put a coarser spin on it. During the second week, Scarlet intended to treat herself to a little bit of sight-seeing. Crossing a few more items off her bucket list, namely, visiting the Alamo and seeing the state capitol building was an exciting prospect. If she felt up to it, she also wanted to climb Enchanted Rock, a huge pink granite mountain just north of Austin.

Scarlet had shared her fun plans with Annalise. Of course, Annalise knew nothing of her kidney problems or the bucket list. And she never would. Not if Scarlet could help it, at least not until it was all over.

Despite the doctor's recommendations, Scarlet did not intend to seek a transplant from a living person. Surprisingly, the decision hadn't been difficult. Putting another person's life in danger was not something that she could bring herself to do. She would rather die first, which was a high probability, for there were tens of thousands of people on the deceased donor transplant list. You could literally be on the list for years before an opportunity for a transplant arose. And Scarlet didn't have years to spare.

Her reticence to ask for a transplant from someone she cared about stemmed from an incident involving a brother and sister at her church. The sister had been sick for years, and when the time had come when a transplant was a necessity, her brother had willingly made the sacrifice. The sister had come through with flying colors. The brother, the donor, was another story. He had died on the operating table. Scarlet would never forget this, and she would never risk the same thing happening to someone she cared about.

While driving through the dense forests near Crockett, Scarlet's thoughts turned to Alex. Annalise had said that he was very handsome, and that he had more girlfriends than he could count. She had heard the wistful tone in her sister's voice. Annalise had a matchmaking streak a mile wide, and Scarlett knew that nothing would make her happier than attempting to fix her little sister up. Scarlet had begged Annalise not to say anything to Alex. She would rather get there and evaluate her own chances. Annalise would never understand that Scarlet wasn't looking for a date or for a boyfriend, she just wanted to experience sex with someone that she didn't have to be afraid of.

* * * *

Alex was having a bad day. He sat in the office of *The Lost Maples* and listened as his chief engineer explained to him why they had to disappoint their best customer. Rick LeBeau had worked for Alex for over a year in his eco-conservation consulting firm. It had come as a surprise to find out that Rick knew Ethan's fiancé, Annalise. She didn't remember him, but he definitely remembered her. Rick had lived in a neighboring community, but they had gone to the same small high school. This meant that he also knew Annalise's elusive sister, Scarlet.

At first, Alex had been intrigued by what Lise had told him about Scarlet. And he would have to admit that he had temporarily entertained a fantasy or two about her. After all, Scarlet was a sexy name, and if she looked anything like her sister, Scarlet would be a knockout.

Emotionally, Alex was ready for a meaningful relationship. Ethan and Annalise were so happy that Alex had begun daydreaming about finding someone who would love him as much as Annalise loved his brother. So when he had found out that Annalise had a sister, and that she would be coming for the wedding, he had begun building this impossible image of the unknown woman. He had pictured her in his mind, how she would look, how she would move, how she would kiss.

But then Rick LeBeau had blown that all out of the water. Apparently, Scarlet was nothing like Alex had imagined her. The more he learned about Scarlet, the more his mental image of her changed. So far, he had found out that she was the town librarian and the office manager at the little Lutheran church. Alex knew he was stereotyping, but how sexy could a librarian/church worker be?

Annalise had also told him of Scarlet's plans to take

in the tourist stops in the hill country. As bad as he hated to admit it—and Alex could see it coming—*he* was going to be the one that got roped into taking the little church mouse around sight-seeing. At that thought, Alex felt guilty. The term 'church mouse' wasn't his nickname for Scarlet, it was Rick's, but he had found himself thinking of her that way more than once. The church mouse. He could see her now. She would be plain—nondescript hair, pale eyes and a figure that wouldn't garner a second look. Not exactly fantasy material, despite Annalise's glowing description. Alex knew that a sister's love was often blind.

Trouble always comes in threes, and here was problem number two. Like icing on the cake, now, there was trouble with the wedding preparations. Alex didn't know how he came to be in charge of it all, but that was how it had worked out. Early this morning, the bakery where Annalise had ordered the wedding cakes had burned to the ground. He couldn't wait to share *that* little bit of information. Annalise would go nuts. To make matters worse, the caterer had called and they were having trouble with the menu the bride and groom had requested. Suffice it to say, Alex was in a shitty mood.

So, when Annalise had told him that her sister was coming ten days before the wedding, he had struggled to hide his displeasure from her. With everything he had to do, he certainly didn't have time to baby-sit company or entertain some backwoods country bumpkin.

Alex realized he was being mean, and this just wasn't like him. By the time Scarlet arrived, he promised himself that he would be over it and on his best behavior—but for right now, his true feelings were bubbling to the surface.

Seeing Rick out, Alex realized that he hadn't heard half what the man had said. Not that it would make any difference in this case. Rick was a strange one. He was always in CYA mode. Cover your ass. The man was paranoid and carried a small digital tape recorder with him everywhere he went. Alex laughed to himself. He supposed he was lucky that Rick didn't use one of those fancy cell phones to video tape everything. He supposed it did keep down confusion for Rick, but it was still a little on the creepy side.

Emphasizing the necessary outcome with their top customer, Alex blew out a long breath, feeling frustrated. "Bottom line, just do whatever it takes, Rick," he instructed his employee.

"Will do. And you be careful of that church mouse. Desperate women can be hazardous to your health." The stocky, balding engineer smirked as he added yet another jab against Annalise's sister. To tell the truth, Rick was beginning to get on Alex's nerves. Enough was enough. He hated to waste a day hanging out and waiting on a wedding guest who was coming way too early and staying way too long, but that was just how it was and he couldn't help it. But none of it was any of Rick LeBeau's business. His employee's poor attitude made Alex want to improve his own outlook. He had no intention of hurting Annalise, he thought too much of her.

As Rick drove away, another car passed his, heading his way. Maybe, this was Scarlet, and he could get on with his day. No, Alex recognized this car. It was the shapely, eager Sandy Moffett. Raking a large, strong hand through his unruly curls, Alex sighed. "Crap!" He wasn't in the mood for Sandy, either. What he needed to do was talk to his brother. Vent a little. He rolled his eyes heavenward and wondered what he had done to piss off the powers that be.

"Alex, I'm so glad to see you!" A cloud of expensive perfume nearly choked him as Sandy launched herself at him.

"Easy, darlin." Alex attempted to extricate himself from the amorous grasp of the overly enthusiastic blonde who was attached to him like a grass burr on a cat's tail.

"When will you go out with me again, Alex?" Sandy Moffett whispered the question as she maneuvered herself up two levels on the front steps of *The Lost Maples B&B*. "Now, I'm on your eye level, you sexy hunk."

Alex was standing on the ground with his back to the parking lot. Her arms were around his neck and it would appear from the rear that they were locked in a heated embrace. Alex hoped Ethan or Bobby didn't show up, he wasn't in the mood for any damn teasing. Sandy was a girl he had dated a few times. She worked at the county clerk's office and he had met her through a mutual friend, the county judge.

"I don't know, Sandy. We have a wedding here in just a few days, and there is a butt-load of company coming in." He had his hands on her arms, steadily trying to loosen her grip on him. This little woman was strong!

"Can I come to the wedding?" Sandy looked up at him expectantly with bright green eyes, their not quite true-to-life shade came courtesy of colored contact lenses.

"No, Sandy. This wedding is mostly family. Invitation only. Look, why don't you come over in a couple of days, we'll throw a few steaks on the grill, just you and me."

"Promise?" Sandy pouted, her plump lips parting slightly, waiting for his kiss.

"Promise." Alex wasn't tempted in the least. He loved women and he certainly loved sex, but right now he had too much to do and not enough time to do it in.

After a little more persuasion, he finally got Sandy Moffett off the property.

Whew! After she had left, Alex walked around the outside of the B&B, checking the flower beds, picking up a stray pecan limb. If he only knew the time of Scarlet's arrival, he could have planned his day more effectively. He had been surprised to learn from Annalise that Scarlet didn't have a cell phone. Who doesn't have a cell phone these days? So, he was reduced to waiting. And waiting. Frankly, Alex was ready to meet her, greet her, get her safely ensconced in a guest room and go about his business, forgetting that she was here.

Out of the blue, his cell rang. Alex looked down, it was Ethan. Thank God.

* * * *

The drive had been incredible. Scarlet very rarely got to leave East Texas and she thoroughly enjoyed the road trip. She had sung with Elvis, drank an icy cola, and bought a loaf of Jalapeno cheese bread at a smokehouse in Centerville. It had been great! Inexpensive, to boot.

She turned down Lonely Street and broke into her rendition of Heartbreak Hotel, imagining the comparison. Annalise had said that Ethan and Alex had not booked any guests for several weeks, not until she and Ethan could get back from their honeymoon in Hawaii.

Rounding a curve, the Bed and Breakfast came into view and Scarlet was instantly entranced. It was absolutely beautiful. The grounds were covered in large oaks and pecans that were now in their full fall colors. Flowerbeds were overloaded with plants of every description and a garden full of antique roses was putting on its last show of the season. Whoa! All of the natural beauty put together wasn't as eye-catching as what stood on the front walk. "Be still my heart," she whispered. Scarlet knew what Ethan looked like, Annalise had e-mailed her a picture of him. The only photo that she had seen of Bobby was in his football uniform, but she knew that he had dark hair. So, the man standing before her had to be Alex. Scarlet realized that her sister was the worst kind of liar. Alex was not good-looking, he was breathtaking. He had to be at least six-foot three, with a body sexy enough to make any woman drool. His shoulders were as wide as a city-bus. And his hair, swear to God, it was golden and hung in wavy curls that almost touched his shoulders. No, this man wasn't good-looking, he was Greek God Gorgeous.

Scarlet instantly abandoned her plan to ask Alex to make love to her. Completely and without reservation she laid it aside. There was no way in hell that she could ever seduce this man. Lord, she wouldn't even know how to start.

Scarlet didn't do well around good looking men. She had learned a trick, however. Scarlet Evans could almost make herself invisible. If she were a superhero, invisibility would be her power of choice. Since that wasn't possible, she used the mask approach. When she wore the mask, no one could see the real Scarlet, she could go about her business, bothering no one and getting in no one's way.

Here was the updated plan. She would be nice, she would be helpful, and she would be gracious. And no one would ever have to know that she had ever had a single sexual thought about Alex or anyone else. Scarlet Evans could pull off asexuality with finesse.

After she had parked, she eased the car door open, not wanting to disturb his phone call. He was standing with his right profile to her, and thankfully as she got out, he shifted to where his back was completely to her. Carefully, she removed the big box out of the back seat that contained Annalise's wedding dress. She tiptoed behind Alex and sat it down on the grass. She was about to return to the car for the rest of her things when she heard him.

Honestly, she wasn't trying to eavesdrop but he was right there. She immediately wished that she was anywhere else.

"I know, Ethan. It's just that having to be stuck with Scarlet is going to make all of this freaking difficult. What are we going to do about the cakes? No, don't tell Annalise. I'll figure something out. I know. I'm sure Scarlet is a very nice girl, but come on—we can't possibly have anything in common. What will we talk about? She'll probably be drooling all over me and Bobby. My chief engineer went to high school with her and he said that everyone calls her 'the church mouse'. She's always making things for people, my engineer says, in hopes that it will make people like her better. I wonder what she made for us. Anyway, he said that she's sort of pitiful, an old maid in the making, the town spinster. And you know how dangerous women like that can be. Sex starved and lonely. I know, I know. I'm just talking to you. I would never say any of this around Annalise. I love her. But good grief, Scarlet is coming for two weeks! Couldn't she have just come for the wedding and then left? And the two of you will be gone after Saturday and I'll be forced to spend all of that time with her! By myself! Can you imagine what torture that will be? All right. I'll get a grip. She should be here sometime today. When is Annalise coming? Well, good. Maybe, she will be here to meet Scarlet and I can avoid her as long as possible." Alex turned slightly sideways. A movement caught his eye. Then he saw her. "Shit! Someone's here. I've got to go." He closed the cell phone and Scarlet wished she could disappear.

"Excuse me? Sorry, you had to hear that. The Bed and Breakfast isn't open for the next couple of weeks. You can make a reservation for a later date if you'd like. We have a wedding planned. My brother is getting married. I'm rambling, forgive me. You just took me by surprise. If you could give me your number, I could send you some coupons for a discount on your next visit."

Scarlet stood still for a moment, not really sure what to do. His words had cut her like a knife. The hurtful moniker surprised her. Who did they know that would call her by that name, the church mouse? She had hoped that she could escape her regular life, just for a little while. It seemed that it had caught up with her. It was obvious that Alex did not realize who she was. For a moment, she considered just leaving, but she couldn't do Annalise like that. As he talked, she closed her eyes and willed herself not to cry. Her chest was aching and tears were burning the back of her throat. On top of all that, she realized that she was trembling. Shutting her eyes tight, she sought calm. Calm.

Apparently, she must have delayed a bit too long. She heard him clear his throat. Raising her eyes to meet his, there was no way to hide the tears that shone in them, or the way her thick lashes were spiked with moisture. What could she do? She had to think of some way to save face for both of them.

* * * *

Wow. When he had looked around it had been a shock. Standing behind him, with the biggest, saddest eyes he had ever seen, had been the most beautiful woman he had ever laid eyes on. Lord, she was gorgeous. He had rambled like a two-bit radio—just couldn't hush. But damn, this woman was hot! He hated that she had heard him spouting off, he liked to make a good first impression. Maybe, he could get her number before she left. Had he actually offered her coupons? Sexy move, Stewart.

But, when she raised her head and looked at him. Alex realized something was wrong. Why was the lovely girl crying? She must be really disappointed. For a moment, he considered making an exception and renting her a cabin anyway.

She looked so familiar. Did he know her? Then, the truth hit Alex like a ton of bricks. He let out a harsh, ragged breath. Dammit! She looked like Annalise! "Scarlet?" This beautiful creature was Scarlet? "God, I'm so sorry." Alex couldn't breathe. What had he done?

He watched her face change, just as if she was pulling a mask into place. Standing up straighter, clearing her throat, she smiled a small smile. Obviously, she was doing her best to salvage the awful situation. With a sinking heart, he watched her hold out her hand in greeting. "Hello, Alex. It's a pleasure to meet you. Annalise speaks so highly of you." Hell, she was trying to put him at ease.

Alex was so shocked, he couldn't move. Scarlet's hand wavered, then Alex realized how much worse it would be if he let it drop, untaken. Accepting her little hand into his large one, he was amazed to feel a sensual current as real as any electrical charge pass between them. She pulled her hand from his and put it behind her, confusion darkening her eyes.

Feeling like a fool and not knowing what to say, Alex began to speak, anyway. "Scarlet, please let me apologize. It's no excuse, but I've been cranky as hell. Everything that could go wrong has gone wrong, and I was taking it out on you. Please…I'm so sorry." He had never felt like this before, as if something beautiful had slipped through his fingers and now lay shattered in a million pieces on the floor. His eyes took her in. She was not just beautiful, she was delectable. Wearing simple, soft, faded blue jeans and a pink lace camisole, she was completely and utterly feminine. Her long brown hair was captured in a braid that hung halfway down her back. There was a definite similarity to Annalise, in their coloring and in their expression. But she was very different, wonderful, in ways that he couldn't put his finger on. Standing no more than five three or four, she was perfectly, exquisitely curved. And God in Heaven, she wasn't wearing a bra. His eyes followed the gentle swell, the hint of a dusky pink nipple peeking through the lace.

She stepped back from him slowly, talking all the while. "It's all right, Alex. Don't think another thing about it. Eavesdroppers never hear well about themselves. Besides, everything that you said about me is true, except I'll be very careful not to drool on you, or Bobby. The good news is that there has been a change in plans." She smiled at him weakly, still backing up. "I've decided it would be smarter if I got a hotel room in town, close by a fabric store. That way, it will save me trips into town to buy things that I need for the dresses that I'm trying to finish. I really only stopped by to do a fitting on my sister, then I'll be on my way. Do you think I could see her, please?" By the time she had finished speaking, she had put at least ten feet between them.

"Dresses? What dresses?" Alex couldn't think straight. He couldn't take his eyes off of her face. She was everything he had initially dreamed she would be. And stupid oaf that he was, he had ruined it before she even walked through his door. A lump formed in his throat as he watched her quickly swipe a few tears from her face. Alex winced at the fact that Scarlet was doing her best to hide the hurt that she was feeling. Hurt that he had inflicted. Alex's chest tightened. He wasn't used to hurting small, precious things.

"I've made the bridal gown and the maid of honor gown, but they still need to be fitted." He had to lean over to hear her voice. It had dropped to an almost indiscernible level. To his dismay, he saw that Scarlet couldn't bring herself to meet his eyes. Instead, she worried her full bottom lip with her teeth, all the while studying the interesting details of the sidewalk.

"God, Scarlet. I had no idea you were sewing the gowns. No wonder you needed to come early." Alex mentally castigated himself for his stupidity. In all of his years, he had never been so clumsy with someone else's feelings. Cursing himself, he racked his brain for the words to say to make it better. "Come inside with me, please. Annalise should be here any minute. And no one wants you to leave. You are more than welcome to stay with us. I want you to stay here with me."

She was unfailingly polite, but adamant. "Thank you, but I'm sure it would be better if I stayed in town. It's such a lovely day and you have a fabulous yard. Would it be all right if I waited out here?" She motioned to a nearby bench.

"Of course." He looked over at her little car. It was obvious that she had intended to stay at *The Lost Maples*, her luggage was sitting beside the left back tire.

She left all of the boxes where they lay and made her way to the rustic wooden bench. Alex followed. When she realized that he was aiming to join her, she blanched. "Oh, please. Don't feel like you have to baby-sit me." He noted her use of his unfortunate choice of words. "I don't mind waiting alone. Please, go and do whatever you'd be doing if I weren't here. I promise that I'll stay out of your way." She wasn't being coy or sarcastic. Alex could tell that she was truly contrite, thinking that her small presence in his life was causing him problems. Alex felt like the biggest heel in the world.

He sat down by her, feeling her draw up and scoot to the very, far edge of the seat. Alex bent over, holding his head in his hands. For a moment they sat in silence. "Scarlet, I love your sister as if she were my own. I would do anything in the world for her. If she finds out that I've made such a mess of things with you, she is going to be devastated."

* * * *

For a few moments, Scarlet didn't know what to say. Her chest felt funny, and she was having problems getting a deep breath. Her skin felt tingly from just being close to this incredible man. Scarlet realized that she needed to say something, but all she could think about was getting back into her car and putting as much distance between herself and Alex as possible. Thoughts of the bucket list, seducing Alex, taking joy in being a part of a real family for a few days—all of this flew right out of her mind. She just wanted out of here! But, what about Annalise? She hated to disappoint her sister.

Lifting his head, he turned his big body until he could look her in the eye. "Is there any way in the world that we can start over?" She could tell he was sincere, and what the heck, she had nothing to lose. She could afford to be nice. In fact, considering that she might be meeting her maker, sooner rather than later, it might pay to turn the other cheek as the Good Book required. Bucking up her courage, she gave him a real smile. "All right. But, please don't feel bad because my staying here isn't convenient. I'm sure that Annalise will be fine with my staying in town." Scarlet refused to think about the cost. She would deal with it, somehow.

Before she knew what was happening, Alex knelt

in front of her. It was odd, but every muscle in her body was clamoring to get close to him. She had to stiffen her joints, just to stop the reflexive action of reaching out to pull him close. This was highly unusual, she just didn't react to men this way. It was going to take all of her strength to act normal around him. Never, ever, must she let him realize she was attracted to him. But what he had to say touched her heart.

"I want you to stay. After all, this is a B & B, we have more than enough room." He slowly reached out and rubbed one strong finger down the back of her hand. "Please, Scarlet."

Her breath caught in her throat. Nervously, she let her tongue move over her lips. "If you're sure it won't be too much of an imposition. I never meant to be a burden. And to clarify a point, I always intended to leave the day after the wedding. Actually, I have reservations and an itinerary. It never crossed my mind to ask you to show me around or take me anywhere, really."

Taking her hand in his, he entwined their fingers. She watched their hands, mesmerized. "Sweetheart, everything that I said before was a pile of crap! I've stupidly hurt you with words that meant absolutely nothing. I was frustrated with other people and little things that were going wrong. I was just spouting off. Please say that you can forgive me and forget I ever said any of those hateful words." He looked so sad, her heart went out to him.

"There's nothing to forgive. And life is much too short to dwell on unhappiness. Let's pretend it never happened. You're very important to Annalise, and I'd never want to do anything to make any of you uncomfortable."

"So, you'll agree to stay in the main house, with us, like you originally planned? None of this talk about going to a motel or anything?"

Scarlet answered very carefully. "Only if you're absolutely sure." She stopped talking. Dizziness washed over her. "Alex, could I trouble you for a glass of water?" Scarlet felt like her blood pressure was through the roof, and her mouth was so dry, she felt like her lips might be cracking. She knew that these were warning signs that soon she ought to lie down and take it easy, but there was too much to do. Living with kidney problems was a hassle.

"What's wrong? Do you feel sick?"

His voice was gentle and sweet, making her want to lean into his magnificent body and make herself at home. "No, I'll be fine. It was a long drive, that's all." She wasn't about to tell him her problems, pity was one thing that she could live without. And now that she had accepted the foolishness of even considering a sexual connection with him, there would be no reason for him to know any of the shameful details.

* * * *

Alex was up like a shot. A few moments later, he was back with a tall glass of iced water. "Here, love. Drink this." This was pitiful. Here he was, a man who made a good portion of his living being a good host, and he had treated this sweet girl like an unwanted intruder. First, he had made her feel totally unwelcome, and second, he hadn't even had enough manners to offer her a simple glass of water.

He watched her drink, jealous of the glass that felt the touch of her lips. "Feel better now?"

She took a deep breath and nodded, "Yes, I believe I do." He counted six freckles that played along the bridge of her nose and he saw thick long eyelashes that shyly shielded eyes that he swore were the deepest sapphire blue he could ever remember seeing. He was totally enchanted. Funny. Before, all Alex had been concerned about was avoiding Scarlet. Now, all he could think about were excuses to be around her.

Unexpectedly, she touched him. Covering his hand with her small one, she offered him comfort. "Thank you, I think I will be just fine, now." Much to Alex's dismay, she moved her hand. He searched her face for any sign that she had been coming on to him, but there was none. Damn!

"Since you've decided to stay, can we go in and get you settled?"

"Yes. Of course. I'm sure there are better things you could be doing than sitting with me." She stood up, and swayed, not altogether sure on her feet. Alex reached out a hand to steady her, sorely tempted to just sweep her up into his arms and head for his bedroom.

Instead, he settled for one more touch. Allowing his fingers to trail along her cheek, he got her full attention. "There is no where I'd rather be than with you. You are the sweetest, sexiest thing that I've seen in many a day, and I fully intend to spend as much time with you as possible." When she didn't reply, he went a little farther. "Are you seeing anybody, Scarlet?"

She stood very still, looking at him closely. Chewing on her bottom lip, she seemed to weigh her words. "Of course not. I'm the church mouse. Remember? The spinster. The old-maid in the making. You thought you were being insulting, but you only spoke the truth. So, please don't think that you have to say things to flatter me. I'm not used to it, and I certainly don't expect it."

Her answer had flowed in a heated whisper. He watched her, she hadn't taken her eyes off of his lips. Seeing her focus, Alex groaned his own hunger. There was no way in hell that he was going to be able to resist her. Placing a hand on the small of her back, he pulled her close. A tender little gasp escaped her throat. "Are the men in your hometown crazy? I'll tell you what the truth is. The truth is that you are totally hot, and if I can't have your lips soon, I'm going to go out of my mind." Their eyes locked, he slowly began to lower his head. He was a fraction of an inch away from her mouth. He was so close, he could taste her breath. Time stood still. Her lips parted, ever so slightly. Alex felt his cock rise to the occasion, knowing that this was going to be the sweetest, most arousing kiss of his life.

They didn't hear the car pull up. They had eyes only for each other.

"Scarlet! You're here!" The bride had arrived.

Alex growled his frustration. Damn! He pulled back, leaving her looking at him with the dreamiest expression that he had ever seen on the face of a woman. She looked at him like she was seeing her first Christmas tree or her first falling star. And he was determined to follow through. There was nothing in the world that would stop him from giving her everything that she wanted. He couldn't keep from smiling, for he knew what Scarlet wanted.

Scarlet wanted him.

Annalise's view of the couple had been hampered by a strategically placed azalea bush. Before she came close enough to make anything out, Alex knew he needed to step away from Scarlet. He had no desire to share their magic with anyone else, not yet.

"I'm going to let you go now, sweetheart. But I want you back in my arms. Tonight."

CHAPTER TWO

Scarlet couldn't breathe. He was standing so close. And, God help her, she wanted to be closer. Heat emanated from his body in waves and it was all she could do to remain upright. It was as if his body was a powerful magnet and she was a helpless, hapless piece of metal, completely vulnerable to his attraction. Had he been about to kiss her? What a thought! All she had wanted was one taste. One taste. Just to see if his lips could possibly be as sweet as they looked.

Suddenly, she had her doubts. This had to be something else. She was so ignorant of the ways of a man and a woman, she just couldn't be sure. It could be part of his apology, trying to make up to her for what she had overheard him saying on the phone. Worse, he could be making fun of her. Like prom. Like any number of incidents over the years, where boys had pretended to like her for a few laughs, for a joke. That was probably it. A joke. And if it was, this was going to hurt worse than anything ever had.

Later, she'd have to thank Annalise for her timely arrival.

"I'm so glad to see you." Her sister enveloped her in a huge hug and Scarlet was equally thrilled to see Annalise. "I'm getting married!" Scarlet laughed as her sister twirled in a state of absolute joy. She exchanged glances with Alex, who was watching his future sister-in-law with affection. He gave Scarlet a private wink. Her heart turned over in her chest. "What are you doing out here? Let's go in. Alex, isn't she beautiful? I told you she was beautiful. Will you get her bags, Alex? Can I see my dress? Oh, I'm so glad you're here." Annalise was talking ninety to nothing, giving no one else a chance to inject a word.

Alex went to get the boxes and luggage, faithfully following Annalise's instructions.

"Isn't he absolutely gorgeous?" Scarlet leaned in to listen as her sister whispered conspiratorially.

"Yes, he is." The truth was the truth. Lowering her voice, Scarlet whispered intently. "Please don't tell him that I'm beautiful. I'm not and it's very embarrassing."

"But you are." At Scarlet's intent, serious stare Annalise relented. "Okay, I won't say it anymore." Putting her arm around her sister, she changed the subject. "How was your drive?"

"Great. I sang all the way."

"Did you practice my wedding songs?" Annalise asked. Alex caught up with them, put the bags down and opened the front door of the B&B.

"You sing?" He looked right at Scarlet. "I can only imagine what your voice sounds like, I bet it's beautiful."

With a flourish, Annalise gestured for Scarlet to step over the threshold. "Welcome to my new home. And yes, she sings like a dream. Deep, throaty, smooth as velvet. I've asked her to sing two of my favorite songs at the wedding, *Unchained Melody* and *Love Me Tender*."

"Elvis." Alex said, knowingly. "I love Elvis."

Scarlet glanced at him with new appreciation. He didn't have to like her just as long as he liked Elvis. Anybody that loved Elvis was okay in her book. Walking into the lobby of *The Lost Maples,* she inhaled sharply. "It's breathtaking. You have a beautiful home." And it was. The B&B was decorated in a Country French flavor, favoring white wood, blue accents with a hint of lemon yellow here and there. "Living here must be a dream come true."

"It is heavenly," agreed Annalise. "Especially being with Ethan." Alex snorted playfully. Turning to glare at him, Annalise promised. "Just wait till you fall in love, Alex. You're going to fall so hard, and I'm going to enjoy watching every minute of it."

While Annalise teased him, he looked right at Scarlet with a hungry, heated expression. It made her heart pound. "You may be right, Lise."

"I can't stand it. I've got to see my dress." Annalise scurried around, hunting the large box that contained her dress.

"Is this what you're looking for?" Alex held it up over her head, teasing her.

"Yes!" She jumped, but he was too tall. He finally placed it into her outstretched arms, giving Scarlet another tender smile. Annalise sat flat out on the floor and opened the box. "Oh. My. God." She jumped up, pulling the ornate gown out the box. Yards and yards of organza and lace flowed from her fingertips. "Scarlet, this is the most beautiful dress I have ever seen."

"It's not completed, yet. There are thousands and thousands of seed pearls still waiting to be sewn on." Scarlet enjoyed Annalise's joy.

"I'm going to go try it on." She dashed from the room, the dress over her arm.

Scarlet started to follow her, but Alex stopped her with a gentle touch. "I'm not an authority on wedding gowns, but that dress looked incredible to me. You're very talented."

"Thank you." Scarlet leveled her gaze on his chest, he was wearing a soft burnt orange University of Texas T-shirt and it molded every luscious muscle of his chest and shoulders. "I enjoyed making it for her. Every girl dreams of wearing a beautiful wedding dress and I'm glad I could make my sister's dream come true."

"Do you dream about your wedding, Scarlet?" Alex's voice was hypnotizing.

Scarlet answered without thinking. Some questions

need to be pondered, this one was easy. "No, I don't dream about my wedding. I won't be getting married."

* * * *

Before he could ask her why she felt that way, she retreated from the room. Her answer had left him speechless, and for some odd reason, strangely bereft. Which was odd. He was allergic to weddings and to brides. Once divorced, he had carefully avoided any and all close proximity to matrimonial affairs—until his brother had been reunited with his soul mate. Now, it seemed different somehow.

A noise at the front alerted him that Ethan was home. Good, he wouldn't be the only man. There was safety in numbers. He met his brother at the door, and together they headed for the kitchen.

"So she heard what you said?" Ethan sat by his brother, pouring himself a steaming cup of coffee.

"Every word." Alex stated matter-of-factly. "That incident has to rank as the stupidest thing I've ever done."

"I wonder why LeBeau fed you that crazy line about Scarlet being plain and mousy?" Ethan and his brother spoke frankly about everything. They were one another's best friend. "She isn't mousy is she?"

Alex looked at his brother steadily. "No, she's stunning. In fact, she is the most beautiful woman I have ever seen in my life. Her face is incredible and her body..." His voice trailed off, leaving himself wide open for Ethan's teasing.

"My God, you're smitten." Ethan grinned, enjoying his brother's predicament.

Alex had to laugh. "Yeah, I guess you could say that." He reached for the pot and freshened both of their cups of coffee. "She has no idea that she's beautiful. I don't believe that anyone has ever told her, before."

"And you have?" Ethan wasn't going to cut his brother any slack. "Already? And you've known her how long?"

"Long enough." Alex had broad shoulders, he could handle anything his brother dished out. "You know, Scarlet is oblivious to the fact that she has anything a man could want."

"I guess you're going to enjoy enlightening her to that fact," Ethan said dryly.

"It's my new mission in life." Alex pulled another chair around, so he could prop up his long, strong legs.

"How long do you think they'll be in there trying on wedding finery? I'm hungry." He was always hungry.

"Till the cows come home." A dry wit ran in the Stewart family.

"We don't have any cows." Some were wittier than others.

"Exactly."

****

"Please don't try to set me up with Alex, Annalise. I'm begging you." Scarlet looked at her sister imploringly.

"By the way he was looking at you, I don't think I'm going to have to do a thing." The bride-to-be carefully hung her wedding dress up on a hanger. Looking over at her sister's determined expression, "I can see the subject is closed—for now. Will you cook for me?"

Scarlet softened. "Of course I will. What do you want?"

"I bought everything for Shrimp Creole and Rum Raisin Bread Pudding."

"Lead the way to the kitchen."

The time that Scarlet had spent with her sister had not been wasted. She had used it to calm her nerves and firm her resolve not to react to Alex's teasing. There was no way he could really be serious about being attracted to her. So the best thing she could do was steel herself against his charm and just be casually friendly. After all, he would soon be her brother, almost. They would be practically family. Of course, she would probably never see him again after this trip. She might not ever see Annalise, again, either. It had taken her months to save up for this vacation, and she knew that soon, she wouldn't feel up to traveling. A wave of sadness washed over her.

Alex and Ethan were sitting at the table. Scarlet's eyes immediately met Alex's. So much for her resolve. She could almost feel the touch of his gaze. He wasn't even trying to hide his interest—if that was what it was.

"Before you leave, you've just got to make me a few batches of cookies. Please." Annalise unashamedly begged.

"Girl, do I have a surprise for you." Scarlet was glad for the distraction. Those gift jars were going to make her sister smile. Running out to the car, she retrieved a heavy bag. Before she could extract it from the car, strong arms reached around her and picked it up.

"What have you got in here, bricks?" Alex smiled at her.

"Cookie mixes in a jar. From scratch. I brought enough so Annalise can satisfy her sweet tooth for a long time." As he walked, he rummaged through the bag.

"Brownies, M&M cookies, Cowboy Cookies, Oatmeal Raisin...damn girl, Annalise won't be eating these by herself."

Reentering the kitchen, she let Alex put up the jars

as Annalise closely examined each one. She watched Alex out of the corner of her eye. He was a bigger distraction than the cookies.

"My baby sister is going to fix us a fabulous home cooked meal." Annalise announced, happily as she bounded into the room.

"Great. I'm starving." Ethan pulled Annalise onto his lap and greeted her with a passionate kiss. "For you."

Scarlet turned away, embarrassed. She began to rummage in the refrigerator, pulling out items needed for the flavorful Creole stew.

"Let me help. I make a great sous-chef." Before, she could turn him down Alex had begun to gather knives, skillets and pots. It was obvious he knew his way around the kitchen.

"This is your kitchen isn't it?" she observed as the obvious truth dawned on her. "I should have asked before I began pilfering through your things."

"Nonsense. Make yourself at home," he handed her a shrimp deveining tool, their fingers accidentally touched. She felt the contact over her entire body. "Can I chop the vegetables for you?"

"Sure." She smiled at him. "I think that a man who can cook is very sexy." Where did that come from? The conversation behind them lulled, Scarlet blushed at her unusual candor.

Alex smiled at her, a bone-melting smile. "Remind me to pick up on this conversation later."

Scarlet made quick work of the shrimp then placed them in cold water until she was ready for them. "Do you have a cast iron skillet?" Alex knew right where to look, pulling one out and placing it on the stove for her. "I make my roux in the oven, how about you?"

"I've always stood and stirred." He watched her combine the oil and flour, and then he set it in the oven to brown. "I like yours way better."

"Scarlet," Ethan interrupted them. "Tell me about your work at the library and the church. How did you happen to combine the two?"

Scarlet finished putting the spices into the tomato mixture.

"I'll finish adding the vegetables, babe." Alex took the spoon from her, as she turned to answer his brother.

"The retiring librarian was a member of my church. She knew me well, and thought I would do a good job at the library. As for the church, one summer the church secretary ran off to get married. I filled in as emergency relief, and gradually it became permanent. I'm fortunate that they are so close in proximity."

"She does everything at the church, except preach." Annalise was on a roll. "She's the pianist, she takes care of the food pantry, runs the church office and best of all she conducts an after-school program for children. They all call her Miss Scarlet."

"Miss Scarlet, huh?" Ethan asked. "So you must be very religious." At his question, both Scarlet and Annalise fidgeted. The soon-to-be newlyweds apparently had not discussed religion, in depth, so Scarlet's answer might come as a surprise.

Scarlet began to talk, ladling the shrimp into sauce. "Our parents were religious. Overly so. In fact, they made our childhood miserable. They talked about religion, but they rarely ever did anything for anybody. I don't talk it, I'm not even sure I actually agree with everything the church believes. But I try to do for other people, especially children."

"Scarlet tries to practice what our parents preached," Annalise started to say something else, but stopped. Then, she started again. "Our dad's dead now, but he was harsh. Especially to Scarlet." Alex's head jerked up at Annalise's words.

"How so?" Ethan asked, curious.

Scarlet sent her a warning glance, but Annalise ignored it.

"Scarlet was born with a club foot."

"That's easily corrected," Alex inserted.

Scarlet blanched with mortification. She hadn't wanted him to know about her deformity. That knowledge always changed things.

"Except he refused to let the doctors fix it," Annalise's voice became bitter.

"He *what*?" Alex's tone betrayed his shock. "I can't believe what I'm hearing. "Your little foot looks perfect."

Scarlet saw him examining her foot. She held it up, and showed him the scar. "When I was sixteen, I was referred to the Shriner's hospital. I was old enough, then, to make my own decisions."

"Why in the world would your father refuse to have your foot corrected?" A harsh note had come into Alex's voice.

"He was crazy," Annalise interjected. "He told Scarlet that God had created her with a club foot, so that must be the way he wanted her to live. He looked upon the deformity as a judgment for her sins."

Alex visibly bristled at the revelation of Scarlet's treatment at the hand of her father. "That was abuse. What sins could the bully have thought this gentle little girl was paying for?"

Annalise turned to her future husband and his brother, continuing to explain. "I know, it was crazy. We had gone to Houston for a consultation on Scarlet's foot the weekend that I was raped."

Ethan shook his head at the horrible memory. "That was the event that caused our six year separation. Misunderstandings and miscommunications almost cost us our love."

"It was partially my fault. I always regretted not

having the surgery sooner. If I had, Lise wouldn't have been alone on the street that night." Scarlet spoke softly and sadly.

"You couldn't have stopped it. They would just have hurt you, too." Painful memories clouded Annalise's face. "Anyway, Scarlet had to live and go to school all of her life with that stupid clubfoot. The kids were cruel and even after she had the operation they still treated her like a pariah."

"I'm so sorry, Scarlet." He placed a hand over hers. Carefully slipping her hand from under his, Scarlet added rum to some raisins for the bread pudding.

"It's over and done with, now."

"Yes. My beautiful sister is as good as new." Scarlet didn't look up at Annalise. She wasn't as good as new. The operation had corrected her foot, but handed her a death sentence when her kidneys were ruined by her bad reaction to the anesthesia. Her parents had decided not to share that bit of news with their oldest daughter. Annalise had soon returned to college, thereby, distancing her from Scarlet and her problems.

Sensing the tension, Ethan tried to change the subject. "So you have a degree in library science?"

Scarlet laughed, "No, my degree is in environmental studies."

"What?" Alex sounded amazed. "I own and operate a conservation consulting firm."

They looked at one another with different eyes. "I bet we have a lot we could talk about." Scarlet thought for a moment. "I knew you were involved in wildlife conservation, Annalise had mentioned your work with the whooping crane."

"Did you bring it?" Annalise asked mysteriously.

At her question, the doubts came back. She remembered Alex's voice as he quoted her nemesis, Rick LeBeau. 'She's always making things for people, thinking it will make them like her better'.

"I'm sure that Alex doesn't want my silly sewing project."

"Yes, he does." Annalise looked at Alex for encouragement.

* * * *

It dawned on Alex that Scarlet had made him a gift, and because of his big mouth, she was hesitant to give it to him. "Scarlet, I would love anything you gave me. Especially, if you made it with your own hands." Because of Scarlet and Annalise's reminiscing, Alex understood a little more now. This went a long way in explaining Rick Lebeau's stupid behavior. He had been one of the cruel kids that had made Scarlet's life a living hell.

A noise in the front room heralded the arrival of another brother. "Hey, Bobby! Come meet Scarlet!" Ethan announced loudly.

Annalise rolled her eyes at Scarlet, "Boys!" was her one word explanation for her future husband's behavior.

"Go get both of their gifts, Scarlet," her sister urged. "And, uh, if you have anything else. Hint. Hint. You can bring that, too."

"What makes you think that I have anything else?" Scarlet teased.

"Well, I've only asked for it for years and years." Alex watched the interplay between the sisters, wondering what Scarlet would bring out. After seeing the intricate work on the wedding gown, nothing would surprise him. He was wrong.

Scarlet came back, literally loaded down with gifts. "Scarlet, this is our brother Bobby," Ethan introduced them.

"Hey!" Bobby stepped forward to give her a hug.

"I'm so glad to meet you, I've heard so much about you." Alex watched jealously, knowing this is how their first meeting could have been if it weren't for his ill-timed tirade.

"Bobby, I've looked forward to meeting you, too. Congratulations on your winning season with the Longhorns." As she offered her compliment, she handed him a tapestry that was about four foot by four foot. Bobby took it slowly, not understanding what she was handing him. "I made it for you. Annalise sent me a photograph of you making a great catch. I used the picture to free-hand the needlework." Bobby held it up, pointing out all of the amazing detail.

"Wow, Scarlet! I see Bevo, the band, the canon—there's even Mack Brown. This is utterly fabulous! I can't believe you made this for me." Once again, he captured her in a hug.

When she turned around to pick up another gift, Bobby looked at his brothers and made a solemn, stage-whispered, announcement. "She's gorgeous. I'm in love." Bobby was kidding, but Alex actually snarled his displeasure.

"Back-off, little brother." Alex was the biggest of the brothers, and right now, he aimed to put the fear of God in his younger sibling. He didn't say, 'she's mine', but the message was crystal clear. The brief exchange was not lost on Ethan or Annalise.

When Scarlet stood in front of Alex, her demeanor was more reserved. He took the tapestry from her hand and held it up. It was the same size and shape as Bobby's. The background was a tree-shaded bayou, and in the center a majestic whooping crane took flight. "I took this photograph one weekend at the Big Thicket national preserve."

Alex had to sit down. He had never been more moved by a gesture. "Scarlet, I don't know what to say.

I have never received a more wonderful gift." He wanted to say more, but now wasn't the time. Annalise was crowding around, anxious to see what her sister had for her and Ethan as a wedding gift.

"Is it what I think it is?" She was practically panting.

"Yes." Scarlet finally gave in and handed her sister a King-size quilt. "A double wedding ring." Ethan had to get up and help his future wife. The quilt was huge and the colors were jewel tones to match the theme in the master suite. "I hope I got the tones right. I'm sure I did, you told me often enough."

As Annalise stuck her tongue out at Scarlet, Ethan examined the small stitches. "I'm impressed, Scarlet."

"My sister can do anything." Annalise announced proudly.

"I think I smell bread pudding." Bobby followed his nose. As everyone pitched in to get the food on the table, Ethan sidled up to Alex. "Have you told 'Lise about the cakes, yet?"

Alex let out a low hiss. "No. As the prospective groom, why don't you do the honors?"

"I guess I have to begin to take some responsibility." As they sat down around the table, Scarlet's Creole dish garnered rave reviews. Finally, Ethan cleared his throat and jumped into the conversation. "Uh, sweetheart," he began.

"Uh-oh, I know that tone." Annalise pierced him with a curious stare.

"Sweetheart, the bakery where you ordered your cakes burned down today." Ethan just threw it out there and then—he dodged.

Alex and Bobby were also very still. Obviously, they expected the worst.

Instead of a hysterical explosion, Annalise calmly turned to her sister. "That French white cake you make with the lemon-raspberry filling…can you make it for a hundred and fifty people?"

"I've done it dozens of times. White chocolate frosting?" Scarlet didn't even act surprised. Her sister nodded. "What type of decorations?"

"White roses and white hydrangeas. And a chocolate ganache grooms cake?"

"I'll have to make a trip into town for pans, tips, tubes and supplies."

"But you'll do it?"

"Consider it done. I'll get what I need tomorrow, that way I can make the flowers and decorations ahead of time. I'll wait till the day before the wedding to actually bake the cakes, that way they'll be fresh." Alex, Ethan and Bobby watched the exchange with mouths ajar.

"Well, knock me down with a feather." Ethan whispered under his breath. "I wasn't expecting calm and reason." Raising his voice to a normal level, he asked Scarlet. "Are you some kind of rural wedding planner?"

"Heavens, no," Scarlet replied, modestly. "I'm just the church lady. For the past four or five years, I've put together every wedding in three counties. I've got it down to a science."

"That's why I wanted her to come early," explained Annalise. "I knew that if anything went wrong, I'd have an expert close at hand. Besides, I haven't got to spend any quality time with you in ages." She ran an affectionate hand over Scarlet's hair, playfully pulling on her braid.

Ethan pinned Alex with a stare. Alex shut his eyes, considering how long it would be before he forgave himself for the way he had treated Scarlet. She had come to help, to sew the dresses and spend a few days with a sister that she hadn't seen in a long time. He looked at

Scarlet, fully expecting her to cast a disparaging look his way. But she didn't. She looked happy. He let out a sigh of relief.

Annalise stood up and began to clear the table. "You two cooked, we'll clean up." She nudged Ethan, who reluctantly agreed.

"I have seed pearls to sew." Looking at Alex, she enquired. "Is there a corner that I can work in? I only need a chair and a bright light."

"My bedroom," he answered with a straight face.

His loaded suggestion didn't faze her a bit. "I wouldn't want to be the cause of you missing your beauty sleep. Is there another place?"

"Sure sweetheart, follow me." He led her to the media room. There were several comfortable chairs and some high-powered lights near the game tables.

"Perfect." She seemed to be more at ease with him, thank God. "Could you show me where you put my things? I think I'll get ready for bed and then I'll work until I can't keep my eyes open." Every word painted a picture in his mind. A hot steamy shower. A soft, silky nightgown. A warm, cuddly woman. "I put you in the room next to mine." No explanation necessary.

She didn't ask for one.

* * * *

Following him, she felt the tingles begin anew. Watching him walk, the movement of his amazing butt in those tight, tight jeans made her tongue grow thick in her mouth. The hall wasn't narrow, but – swear-to-God – his shoulders seemed to brush both walls. He opened the door to her room and let her go ahead of him. He didn't leave her much room, so her body briefly brushed his. She heard his harsh intake of breath. She felt his heat. A dampness began to make itself known between her legs. A totally new experience. Still, Scarlet knew what it was.

After all, she was a librarian.

The room was charming and furnished with comfort in mind. "This is wonderful, Alex. I've never seen a nicer room. It's too much." There was a Queen-sized sleigh bed, a roll top desk, a Lazy-Boy recliner and a roomy armoire. The colors were warm earth tones, highlighted by shades of burgundy and mauve. "This is more than I expected. If you need this room for other guests, I'm used to something much, much smaller."

"Size of the room wasn't the determining factor, love. I wanted you close to me." They stood still, just looking at each other. Electrical currents seemed to arc between them.

"Which bath do I use?" That was a natural question for her to ask, since she was imagining him naked. A vision of him with water droplets all over his body was making her heart pound.

"You have your own, let me take you." Leading her to the oversize bathroom, he showed her the walk-in shower and the claw-foot tub. Stacks of towels, bottles of lotions and salts, everything that anyone could possibly want.

"Alex, I'm not used to luxuries like this. I don't even know what half this stuff is for."

"Do you want me to stay and help?" He sounded as serious as a heart attack.

At that, she laughed. "No, maybe I can muddle through."

"Can I sit with you while you work on the dress?" He asked so sweetly it gave her a warm shiver.

"Sure. I'd appreciate the company." This friendship business wasn't so hard.

"Good." Then he proceeded to knock all thoughts of friendship out of her head. Stepping close, he placed a soft, sweet kiss just to the right of her trembling lips. Every cell in her body commanded her head to turn, just so, so she could move her lips into range for the heady contact. She controlled herself, barely. "I'll be waiting."

* * * *

She was so cute, he could hardly stand it. He hadn't known what to expect when she told him she was going to get ready for bed. Any of his other female acquaintances would have emerged in silk teddies or sheer baby doll pajamas. When she had come out covered in white eyelet from head to toe, Alex had had to reevaluate his whole definition of sexy. The robe was even long-sleeved. The only skin showing was her face, her fingers and her little bare feet. Alex's response to her chaste, angelic outfit was not so pure. He was as hard as the Rock of Gibraltar. It was a good thing he had changed into lounge pants and a loose, long, button-up shirt. It hid a multitude of sins.

He watched her spread the bridal gown out, so the skirt lay in her lap. Opening a round tin, she took out a needle and thread and began to sew on teeny-tiny seed pearls. "What do you do for fun?" she asked him out of the blue.

"I like to go out to dinner and a movie," he answered off handedly, without thinking.

"Is that what you'd do on a typical date?"

He couldn't believe she was asking these leading questions. "A typical date. It could be dinner and a movie or dancing at a club or a picnic at the lake. I've been on many typical dates. How about you? Tell me what you normally do on a date." He watched her work, mesmerized by her nimble little fingers and the way she held her tongue at the corner of her mouth as she worked.

"I've never been on a date." She didn't pause or blink or hesitate.

"You're kidding." The thought that she had never been asked out, escorted to a restaurant, taken care of, coddled or spoiled, just broke his heart. He had a lot of things to make up for. Time was wasting away.

"Think about it. I had a club foot until I was almost seventeen. All of the guys grew up knowing me as the cripple girl. It's like when a fat kid suddenly slims down, it really doesn't matter, no one will ever see them any other way but fat."

"I can't believe your dad did you that way."

"Mom and Dad were strange. Haven't you wondered why our mother isn't coming to the wedding?"

"No, not really. We've never discussed it." Alex took a deep breath and dove in. "Will you go on a date with me, Scarlet?"

"No." It wasn't said harshly, just conversationally.

"Why?" Not that he was taking 'no' for an answer.

"Because, you feel sorry for me. That's why. A pity date would be worse than no date at all."

Alex didn't know what to say. So he just told the truth. "I don't like the way you've been treated. In fact, it infuriates me. I'd like a few minutes alone with every guy that has ever hurt you, including your dad. The pitiful thing is, I'm one of them. I hurt you too. And if I could turn back time, I'd do it in a heartbeat. When you greeted Bobby, so casually and naturally, I wanted to die. Looking back at our first few minutes together, shame just eats me up. A date with you would make me the happiest man in the world. And pity wouldn't have anything to do with it."

Scarlet's hands stilled. "I don't know what to say."

"Say, yes," he coaxed, tenderly.

"I can't. There are things that you don't know."

"Tell me. There's nothing that we can't work out, if we try." He wanted to go to her, but he held himself back.

"Some things can't be fixed, Alex. And I'm not talking about anything you've done or said." She met his eyes. "We're okay. As far as I'm concerned, our first meeting today is irrelevant. You are important to my sister. I'm thankful that she has a family like the three of you. She's very blessed."

"Tell me what's wrong. I promise, before God, that I'll make everything right for you. Let me try, Scarlet. Please, let me try."

With tears in her eyes, she looked at Alex. "I wish you could. You don't know how much I wish you could." All was quiet for a few minutes. They sat companionably. She hadn't said yes to the date. But, then she hadn't really said no, either. Instead, she had issued some kind of a mysterious challenge. And he was just the man to pick up the gauntlet and run with it.

"Tell me what else you do for fun," she pressed.

"I like to play touch football, swim, rock climb, and horseback ride. Basically, if it's outside I enjoy it."

Scarlet blushed, getting a faraway look in her eye.

Alex kept talking. She didn't say anything. "Are you listening to me?"

His amused question seemed to startle her a bit. "What did you say?"

"What's the matter, babe? Are you picturing me all hot and sweaty?"

"Yeah, but you knew that," she said blushing.

Alex was thrilled. She was opening up to him, settling down, even flirting a little. "I like to hear you say it. Turnabout is fair play, what do you like to do for fun?"

She stopped sewing and stared him down. "You wouldn't believe me if I told you."

"Try me."

"When it's late, and dark, I go out into the night…" She whispered, building up the story. Then she laughed. "To the cemetery—with my camera." At his confused look, she clarified. "I ghost hunt."

"Ghost hunt? Like on the Sci-Fi Channel?" He couldn't believe it.

"Yes, but I don't have their level of equipment. I have basic stuff, digital camera, camcorder with night vision, recorders for EVP."

"EVP?"

"Electronic Voice Phenomenon. That's picking up voices on the recorder that you don't hear in real time with your natural ears. Does this freak you out?"

"No, not at all. In fact, I find it fascinating."

She smiled at him. "I can't believe you're being so nice about this. You're really listening, and you're not laughing. Most people don't want to hear me talk about it. They don't believe me. If you're interested I'll show you photographs that I've taken, tell you a few war stories."

"I would love to hear your stories and see your evidence. But, tell me. Why do you do it? It seems like a strange thing for a young woman to be interested in. What's the attraction?" He watched her closely.

"Tonight seems like a night for truth. So, here goes. I'm trying to prove to myself that there's something else out there after we die. I don't really buy the traditional concept of Heaven, so I'm searching."

Alex found everything about Scarlet fascinating. He hung on her every word. She worked tirelessly sewing on the minute pieces of finery. At eleven thirty, Ethan slipped into the room. "Hey, the dogs are going crazy out back. Walk with me and let's see if those pesky coons are back."

Alex didn't want to leave, but duty called. "I'll be

right back."

Scarlet just smiled at him. She looked like she was about to give out. Ten, or so, minutes later, Alex returned. He wasn't surprised to find her sound asleep, cuddled over into a corner of the chair. Carefully, he lifted the wedding gown from her lap and spread it over a nearby sofa. He didn't even consider waking her, he did exactly what he wanted to do. With one hand at her back, and one under her thighs, he lifted her into his arms. Pulling her close to his chest, he stared down at her face. She didn't awaken, instead, she turned into him like a moth to a flame. One hand flattened on his chest, moving up to encircle his neck. Alex tightened his hold on her, pulling her closer in his arms. She reacted instinctively, her mouth seeking out the warm skin of his throat. Alex stopped walking, reveling in her reaction to his nearness. Breathing became secondary, as he focused on the touch of her lips on his skin. A moan of desire rumbled in his chest, and he felt her jerk.

She was awake.

Scarlet opened her eyes. Holy Mother of God! Had she lost her mind? Her lips were on Alex's throat and she was doing a fairly decent vampire imitation. Heavens to Betsy! She was *this* close to giving him a hickey! Mortified, she sought a place of refuge. Burying her face in his chest, she hid from him in embarrassment. "Good Lord, Alex! I'm *drooling* on you. I am *so* sorry! I thought I was dreaming."

"Dream some more, baby. I love how your lips feel on my skin." Alex marveled at her reaction. Even in her withdrawing, she had turned to him. He purposely strode to the wing that housed their bedrooms. Passing up her room, instead, he carried her to his own bed and laid her down. "Sleep with me, Scarlet." His eyes smoldered with a dark promise.

CHAPTER THREE

Sleep with him? Did she hear right? She sat up, looking unsure and a bit alarmed. "Alex, I don't know."

"I said sleep, sweetheart. I just want to hold you. You've got on more clothes than the Flying Nun. Please, let me lay down with you." He began to undress and she couldn't take her eyes off of him. He was magnificently and wonderfully made. Tearing her eyes away, she took off her robe, folding it and laying it on the floor next to the bed.

Undressing completely, except for his briefs, he pulled back the covers. She eased up in the bed, far enough, so she could slide under the covers, too.

"What if Annalise comes looking for me?"

"Ethan will keep your sister occupied. Come here." He held out his arms and she went to him. Laying her head on his shoulder, she molded her body to his. Tentatively, she tested where to lay her hand. Finally, she gave in to her desire, and let it settle on his chest. "Put one of your legs up over mine." She did as he asked, and discovered that they fit together, perfectly. A deep sigh of contentment slipped through her lips.

Alex gave in to temptation and laid his lips on the top of her head, inhaling the clean sweet smell of her hair. "Now, we can rest. I don't understand it, sweetheart, but I couldn't bear the thought of you sleeping anywhere but with me."

"It feels heavenly, being here with you like this." She pushed her body into his, seeking to get as close to him as possible. "Safe and secure."

Scarlet could feel the laughter deep in his chest. "Not exactly the emotions that I want to elicit from a beautiful woman, but, with you? I'll take what I can get." He allowed his hand to rub up and down her back.

She wouldn't know it, not tonight, but this was going to be the sweetest torture imaginable. His shaft was swollen to unbelievable proportions and it literally ached to be buried deep inside of her. But, as far as he could tell, she was blissfully unmoved. She was exhausted. So, tonight he would give her comfort, warmth and security.

Even if it killed him.

When Alex awoke, he was alone. Scarlet was gone. He threw off the covers and stripped off his under shorts. Heading for the shower, he was anxious to do what had to be done, then go and find her when in she walked. No knock. No inquiry. She walked in like she owned the place.

And she did.

"Oh, my sweet Lord." she breathed. "Forgive me for barging in…" her voice trailed off into nothingness. She just stared.

It was morning. He had spent the night, closely intertwined with a woman that he found unbelievably attractive and nature had taken its course.

Alex looked around for something to cover up with. Shocking her would only set their relationship back. He made a grab for his shorts, but she stopped him. "Please don't. You're so beautiful. Please, don't hide from me." Slowly, she walked toward him. "I don't mean to stare, but I've never seen a man before. Only in pictures, and I had no idea." Her words only served to increase his size.

He stepped toward her, unashamed. She held out her hand, almost touching him. Then, as if awakening from a dream, she seemed to realize where she was and the unbelievable thing she was doing. Red heat flashed up into her face, and she whirled around as if to leave. "Stop, Scarlet. It's okay, honey."

"Let me go, Alex. I wasn't thinking. I had no right

to walk in on you like this."

She wouldn't look at him. "I just came to ask you if I could use your laptop to access my recipe files."

Alex pulled her back against him. "No need to be embarrassed. There's nothing here that doesn't belong to you, babe. Where do you think this hard-on came from?" He whispered to her gently. "Snuggling up to your sweet body all night took its toll." He stepped closer to her, letting her feel his massive erection as it nudged her backside. She didn't move away, in fact she leaned back into him.

"I am acting so totally out of character. You must think I'm terrible."

"Does this feel like I think you're terrible?" He let his hips press rhythmically into her tight little ass.

"No, it doesn't." Before she could stop herself, she turned into his embrace, wrapped her arms around his neck and held up her lips to be kissed.

Sending a prayer heavenward, he took the gift that she offered. With a moan of satisfaction, he covered her mouth with his own. She whimpered with joy as he feasted on her lips. "Oh, Alex, this is like tasting chocolate for the first time."

He laughed, truly happier than he had been in a long time. Having her in his arms felt momentous to him, like this was his last first kiss. Accepting his tongue, she learned quickly, giving him back equal portions of passion and pleasure. His cock was nestled between them, and it was all he could do not to rub up and down on her, seeking any sort of relief he could find.

"Scarlet! Scarlet! Where are you Scarlet?" Annalise's voice broke their reverie.

"Damn!" Alex pulled his mouth from hers, letting his forehead rest against the top of her head. "Tonight, I think we'll sleep in my RV. I don't think I'll survive anymore interruptions."

"I need to tell you things." She couldn't tear her mouth away from his face, she kissed his jaw line, his chin, her breathing as erratic as his.

"Nothing you could possibly say would change my mind about how I feel about you." He spoke into her neck, dragging his mouth across her skin, feverishly scraping his teeth along the collarbone.

"Telling you is going to be so hard," she clung to him like a drowning person to a life preserver.

"Scarlet! Are you in there?" Annalise tapped on Alex's door. With a grin, he put a finger over her lips, telling her with his eyes not to respond.

When they heard her footsteps fading into the distance, he pulled her close once again, but this time in a fierce hug. "I've got to get covered up before your sister decides to join us. And yes, you can use my laptop—among other things." Rubbing back and forth sensuously across her belly, he let her know how much he wanted her. "Run out and pacify your sister, then come back and make yourself at home." He pointed at his desk and the computer that sat in the middle of it. Holding her by the shoulders, he stole one more tender kiss, and then with a growl of frustration, he went for the shower.

* * * *

What am I doing? What was I thinking? Scarlet chastised herself as she made her way down the hall toward the kitchen. She couldn't believe that she, Scarlet Rose Evans, Administrator of the First Lutheran Church had just left the company of a naked man with the most magnificent penis she could have ever imagined. She didn't know they came that big! All she could think of was how it would feel for Alex to make love to her.

But she had to tell him about her kidney disease. It wouldn't be fair if she didn't. She had no idea how he would react. How would a man feel about making love to a woman who might not live very long? Talk about a mood killer! Shaking her head, she tried to banish the doubts. Although, she wouldn't blame him if he did decide that he couldn't bring himself to be with her.

"There you are! Where have you been?" Annalise nailed her with a stare. A blush rushed up her cheeks before she could get herself under control. "I knew it! You were with Alex!"

Ethan was coming in the back door and Scarlet was doing everything she could to shush her sister up. "It wasn't like that. We haven't…"

"Ethan!"

"Please don't tell him, Annalise. We haven't slept together, yet. I mean, we've slept together, but we haven't had sex." Scarlet was desperate to shut Annalise up. She didn't want it to get back to Alex that she had been discussing what went on behind closed doors. Finally, it seemed that she got through to her sister. "I've got to go into town and buy supplies for the wedding cake. Any suggestions of a good store?"

"Go into Austin. Alex will take you. There's a great organic grocery and some really good specialty stores that will have exactly what you need." All of this was said with a sneaky grin on her face. Annalise was enjoying Scarlet's discomfort.

"I have no intention of asking Alex to give up a day to take me shopping! Look, I'm about to make a list of things I need, then I'll go on my own." Scarlet escaped the knowing looks of her sister and went to her room to retrieve her papers. As she fled to the safety of Alex's room, her Bucket List fell to the floor. Hastily picking it up, she stuffed it back within the confines of the spiral notebook and did not give it another thought.

This time she knocked. She had learned a lesson, and what a lesson it was. To tell the truth, it was a lesson that she would like to repeat—over and over again.

The door flew open and a hand came out and grabbed her, pulling her into the room and straight into his arms. He picked her up and kissed her like there was no tomorrow. She giggled with delight. "You didn't look to see who you were grabbing. What if it had been someone else?"

"Good thing it was you, I would have hated to kiss one of my brother's like that." He picked her up in his arms and carried her to the desk. Sitting down in the swivel chair, he held her on his lap. "Now, what do you need to look up?"

"Cake and icing recipes and to check and see what size tips I need to make the roses and hydrangeas." She quickly accessed a folder that she kept in her e-mail account. "Can I print this page?"

"Sure." He was busy planting soft, little kisses on the exposed skin at her neck. Reaching around her, he deftly hit send. "When you get ready to go pick up this stuff, I'll take you."

Turning to look him in the face, she checked his expression carefully. "Seriously, you don't have to go. Just map-quest me the street the stores are on and I'll be fine."

"I want to spend the day with you. Come on." Gladly following, she grabbed the print-out, but left the notebook where it lay.

Riding to Austin with him had been wild. They had laughed at childhood memories and he had enjoyed sharing with her points of interest and historical markers. When they arrived at the store, he had helped her gather everything she would need. Now, they were ready to check out and she realized that money might be an issue. She juggled the numbers in her head. It was going to be close. The items she would need to buy today would come close to costing two hundred dollars. Before checking out, Scarlet asked Alex to hold her buggy while she made a quick trip to the restroom. Using the payphone outside the facilities, she cancelled the hotel reservations she had made for the week following the wedding. Without hesitation, she forgot about the Alamo, Enchanted Rock and all of the other places she had hoped to mark off of her bucket list. These changes would free up enough funds to purchase the ingredients, the pans and the decorating items.

Annalise hadn't thought twice about Scarlet paying for the cakes, after all she knew that Scarlet had two full-time jobs. What Annalise didn't know was that the medicine Scarlet took ate up almost all of her salary. Scarlet had also paid for the material for both dresses. And, honest to God, she didn't mind. This was possibly the last thing she would be able to do for her sister and she was glad to do it. Tradition dictated that the bride's family pay for the wedding and she was the only family Annalise had—except for their mother, and frankly, she didn't count.

Returning to Alex, who had been waiting patiently, she headed to the check-out counter. Thankfully, the charges went through on her card and they loaded up. "What else do you want to do while we're in Austin?"

She looked at him, her eyes twinkling. "Annie's ice cream?"

There were five Annie's Ice cream shops in Austin, so Alex had no trouble finding one. "What flavor, babe?"

"The darkest chocolaty chocolate you can find." He laughed at her request, but did his best to fulfill it. "Now what?" He was being so sweet.

"Will you drive by the capitol building?" She knew there would be no overnight trip to Austin after the wedding, so this would have to do.

"Do you want to park and take a tour?"

"No, driving by will do." He did, and Scarlet got up on her knees, so she could see as much of the beautiful building as she could. "It's gorgeous." Alex seemed to enjoy seeing his hometown through her eyes. He drove by the beloved University's forty-acres, pointing out the infamous tower and the huge football stadium where Bobby played. They couldn't drive down Sixth Street, but he showed her what he could and she enjoyed every second, mostly because she was with him. It was at that moment it hit her. Her days with Alex were numbered. Her days were numbered, period. Total dismay clutched her insides like a vise. She wrapped her arms around her middle and tried to hide her sudden inability to breathe.

"What's wrong? Are you hurting somewhere?" Alex looked at her with concern, putting on the brakes, almost coming to a stop. "Do you need to get out of the car? Did the ice cream make you sick?"

"No, somebody just walked over my grave." She really didn't know what that meant, but it sounded good. Attempting to steady her nerves, she focused on the billboards that lined I-35. One caught her eye. "Look, Alex. A Civil War battle display is going to come to Austin!" The Civil War was one of her greatest interests. "I wonder what that's about."

"Are you intrigued by the Civil War?" Alex looked at her sort of funny.

"Obsessed. I read everything I can get my hands on about it. I even have a few artifacts."

Alex ran his eyes up and down her body. "Are you for real?" he asked her, fascinated.

"What do you mean?"

"We have so much in common, it's sort of scary. I love the Civil War. The display that's coming to the capitol next month is one of my pet projects. I'm on the

Austin Historical committee and the Civil War is my main focus. The display you saw advertised is concerning one of the last battles that took place in the war, and it happened at the Palmetto Ranch near Brownsville."

"John Salmon Ford was the commander. He was a Mexican War veteran, former captain of the Texas Rangers and one time mayor of Austin." Her recitation of those little known facts amazed Alex.

"Will you marry me?" He was joking, maybe.

"Don't tempt me," she laughed. "You'll never guess what I have in my collection. Not in a million years."

"What's that?" He stared at her face so hard, she was afraid he'd run off the road.

"I have a presentation sword that was given to Lt. Col Porter Cox in recognition of his killing of Bloody Bill Anderson."

He was suitably impressed. "I know who Bloody Bill was. He sometimes rode and fought with Quantrille's Raiders. How in the world did you get your hands on that? It must have cost a fortune!"

"I don't have any money," she scoffed. "This little old man at church was a first-class Civil War collector. He had no family, and I adopted him, more or less. I visited him every day and when he got sick, I helped take care of him. We spent many hours discussing the siege of Vicksburg, Sherman's march to the sea, Gettysburg—everything you can think of—and when he passed away, he left me the sword."

Alex took her hand in his. "You are a very sweet person." He squeezed her hand. "But, I am so jealous. The sword that killed Bloody Bill Anderson!"

"If I'd known you were into the Civil War, I would have brought it to show you."

"I would love to see it. You can bring it next time,"

Alex said with confidence.

Next time.

She knew there would be no next time.

"Let's go home, sweetie." He brought her hand to his lips and she almost cried.

* * * *

It was a good thing the kitchen at Lost Maples was huge, because Scarlet needed every square inch. Delicate roses and hydrangeas made of tasty fondant were spread out everywhere. Twice, Scarlet had snuck out and lay down for just a few minutes. She was careful to not let anyone know that she wasn't feeling well. Annalise was on cloud nine, and Scarlet was determined she would do nothing to put a damper on the excitement.

Alex had company business to take care of, but he had kissed her before he left and whispered in her ear that he couldn't wait to come home to her. Their trip to Austin that morning had been a revelation for Scarlet. Alex's interest in her was real. She didn't understand it, but it was. He had been sweet, attentive and truly interested in everything she had to say. It hadn't been a real date, it had been too rushed. Hurrying back to work on wedding preparations had curtailed the time they had to spare, but still, it had been wonderful. Plus, she wasn't blind, she could see he had been in almost a constant state of arousal when they had sat close in his burnt orange Hummer. Alex wanted her. That was a heady thought.

Finally, every flower was made and had been carefully boxed up in anticipation of gracing the three-tiered wedding cake. There was even a chocolate longhorn to grace the groom's cake, in honor of Ethan and Annalise's alma mater. Her sister had taken pity on her and had volunteered to clean up the kitchen.

There was no slowing down, however, more seed pearls were waiting to be sewn on and there was a little more work to be done on the maid of honor's dress. Cecile Fairchild, the maid of honor, was Annalise's agent. The steamy romance novels that came from Annalise's fertile imagination had kept both of them hopping for years. Scarlet had never met Cecile and she was anxious to do so. It was important to Scarlet that Annalise have friends and loved ones who would be with her for years to come.

The media room seemed too lonely, so she went to the family room and sat down under a wide window which let in ample light. Sitting on the floor, she leaned back against the wall and settled in for several hours work.

"There's my girl." At the sound of his voice, Scarlet's heart warmed. She looked up at him, always amazed anew, at how truly handsome he was. Joining her on the floor, he claimed her lips in a hard kiss. "You're wearing your hair down," he ran his fingers through the curls that hung almost to her waist. "I love your hair. It's going to look gorgeous spread out on my pillow." Ripples of awareness flowed over Scarlet's body causing her nipples to pebble.

"You left this on my desk." Scarlet looked at what he had in his hand. It was her notebook.

"Wait." She started to reach for it, but it was too late.

"I found this odd list. Scarlet, do you have a tattoo?" He had her bucket list in his hand. It was out of order, but if he kept looking, he would find out that her number one desire had been to seduce one Alex Stewart. Scarlet didn't know whether to cry or run.

"Yes."

"Where?" Swear to God, he licked his lips.

"On my bottom." He closed his eyes and sighed.

"What is it?" He still had his eyes closed.

"A red rose, like my name, Scarlet Rose." What was it with men and tattoos?

"You have a little red rose on your butt? Let me see." He was as serious as a heart attack.

"No!" she huffed. Then she laughed.

"Just a peek?" He was so darned cute. Scarlet rose to her knees and turned her back to him. Pulling her jeans down a little ways, she held the back open so he could glance down on her hip.

Alex groaned. "Damn!"

Scarlet sat back down, quickly, once again reaching for the list. "Not so fast," holding it over her head. "There may be more interesting stuff on this list." He began to peruse it, chuckling here, asking questions there. "What is this list, anyway? A glorified to-do list?" Before she could answer he had shuffled the papers so that the first page was on top. "Bucket list–100 things to do before I die." That wasn't enough to cause him to question, until his eyes rested on the first item.

"Make love." His eyes flew to hers. "Scarlet, what's my name doing here? And it's crossed out." He looked back down at the paper. "Escort service. And it's marked out"

He turned the papers over, reshuffled them and looked at her hard. "Explain. Did you come here looking for sex? If not from me, from a gigolo? I don't understand." Scarlet paused, just looking at him, trying to determine if he was angry.

"I wanted to know what it was like to make love with a man. Just once." There was no inflection in her voice, she wasn't looking for sympathy.

"Why is my name crossed out?"

"It was just a day dream, the whole list is mostly just a wish list. When I got here, I realized that I couldn't go through with it. I changed my mind."

"Why, because of the stupid things I said?"

"No because you're so beautiful." She looked down, unable to watch his face, afraid of what she would see.

"I'm glad you ditched the escort service idea, that's just stupid. Why didn't you want to take the time to find someone and cultivate a relationship with them?" Scarlet blanched. He was talking as if he had never held her close, never whispered warm suggestive words to her that had turned her insides to mush.

Time to come clean. Regardless of the outcome, she owed him an explanation. She would just have to get his promise that what he learned would go no further. "I don't have time to cultivate a relationship."

"You don't have time." He acted like he didn't believe her. "You're too busy to learn to love somebody." Alex was disappointed in her, she could tell.

"It's not so much that I'm 'busy—don't have time...'" Scarlet's voice was soft, but serious. "More like I'm running out of time." At his look of confusion, she clarified. "It's a bucket list, Alex."

"A bucket list?"

"Things I want to do while I'm still—all right." She spoke slowly.

A dawning comprehension cleared his eyes. His tone dropped from irritated to panicked. "What are you saying? Are you sick?"

"The operation that corrected my foot had complications. They gave me the wrong anesthesia and my kidneys were damaged. It's been seven years, and they've progressively weakened. Soon, it will be dialysis, a transplant, or…or…" she stopped talking.

"No, no, no." He pulled her up in his arms and held her close. His arms didn't give an inch, he only tightened his grasp until he was practically squeezing the breath from her body. "Tell me that there's some mistake. Tell me that you're getting back at me for my cruelty."

His immediate and intense reaction melted Scarlet's heart. Her arms crept around his neck and she rubbed her face against his. His face was wet! Oh God, he was crying. "I'm sorry, Alex. Please don't cry."

He pulled back and took her face in his hands, framing it. Rubbing his lips over her eyelids, he kissed her eyes closed. Punctuating his words with kisses, he whispered. "I'll do it. I'll do it. I'll do it. I'll make love to you." He kissed her cheek. "Scarlet, I want you. God, I want you so bad. I've wanted you from the moment I saw you, but now…" He gently pushed aside Annalise's dress and pulled her onto his lap. Shaking his head as if to clear his thoughts, he looked her in the eye. "I want to know everything, baby. I'm so sorry you've had to go through this. When do you start your dialysis?" He was talking so fast, she couldn't get a word in edgewise. When he stilled and waited for her response, her words froze in her throat. When she didn't answer right away, he tilted up her chin to look into her eyes.

"I can't do dialysis. I don't have any insurance." She looked down, then up into his eyes.

He wasn't responding. Disbelief stole his voice. Trying desperately to comfort him, yet explain, she continued, "That's why I'm working at the library and the church. When I graduated college, I couldn't get a job in my field, because I couldn't pass the physical. Their insurance plans wouldn't accept me because I had a pre-existing condition. I work two jobs and take in sewing so I can afford the medicine, but there won't be any dialysis and there won't be a transplant."

* * * *

Alex stood up in a rush. He began pacing the floor. "The hell there won't," he shouted. "The alternative is unthinkable." Alex's mind was whirling. He was a take charge kind of guy and he wasn't about to sit around and watch this precious woman die, not if he could do anything about it. He didn't know what he was going to do. But, by God, he was going to do something.

"How about your family?" Alex was grasping for solutions.

"Dad was a match, but mother and Annalise aren't. And Alex." Scarlet warned in a voice that brooked no argument. "Annalise doesn't know and I don't want her to know."

"What do you mean? She has to know. How could you even consider keeping something like this from your sister?" Alex stood with his hands on his hips, he didn't know whether to spank her or cuddle up to her and never let her go.

"I've kept it from her for seven years. She doesn't have to know, not until…"

Alex couldn't believe this. Every word that came of her mouth tore another hole in his heart. She had been so alone! She had been bearing this burden all alone! "What? Until someone notifies her about the time and the place for the funeral?" The words seemed to cause Alex physical pain. "Who's going to take care of you?"

"I'll take care of myself," she emphasized sternly, lifting her little chin. Alex marveled at her fearlessness. His little soldier.

"What about the transplant list?" Why was he just now thinking of this? His mind wasn't working worth a flip. His divorce hadn't caused even an iota of stress compared to what he was feeling today.

She didn't answer him. He asked again. "You *are* signed up for a transplant, aren't you?" He was still desperately searching, trying to come up with an answer.

"I'm on the deceased donor transplant list, but the chances of that happening before my time is up are about a million to one." She wished she had never made the stupid bucket list. The agony on his face was tearing her to bits.

"How about a living donor, other than your sister? Has everyone else been tested?"

"You are so sweet." Walking over to him, she framed his face. "There is no one else, there will be no living donor, baby. Let's talk about something else."

Picking her up, he kissed her neck, sucking gently. "I'm not giving up, I just need to think. But, right now. I want to make love to you." He started walking toward her bedroom.

She laid her head on his shoulder, resigned. "No. I can't. Not now. I've changed my mind."

"I'm not letting you change your mind. Give me a couple of hours to get the RV ready and packed. Gather a few things and tell your sister that we'll see her this time tomorrow. We're leaving. No argument." Another hard kiss and he was gone.

* * * *

She did as he asked. It wasn't hard. She wanted to make love to him more than anything else in the world. Still, she was more nervous than she could ever remember being in her life. Annalise hadn't seemed surprised. In fact, she had seemed thrilled. "This is what I dreamed of. I love you so much, baby sister. And I love Alex more than I can say. You're perfect for one another."

"Don't read more into this than it is."

"What is it? Just sex? Don't tell me that. I've seen how he looks at you. And I've certainly seen how you look at him. The two of you stare at one another like you're starving." Annalise was adamant in her belief.

"Just don't make a big deal out of this, please."

When Scarlet walked out the front door to meet Alex, she was flabbergasted. RV was a term that could apply to a multitude of vehicles, Alex's was a monster. Forty-two feet of pure, unadulterated luxury. He opened the door with pride and invited her inside. "We use it mostly for tailgate parties at the Texas games."

Scarlet looked around in wonder. She had never been in a more luxurious place. The B&B was fantastic, but this was out of this world. Everything was white and cherry wood, recliners, wet bar, granite countertops, huge plasma TV. There was even a fireplace. "Wait till you see the bed. It's a California King. We have plenty of room to play."

Scarlet stilled. She turned to him, big, huge Teddy bear of a man. Curls of gold that she longed to sink her fingers into. "You don't have to do this, you know. It's okay. I would understand. Making love to a person with…uh, problems has to be a turn-off." She had thought about this. What if he couldn't? What if he got so far, then he had to stop. She would die. Better not to start it at all.

With one swift move, he pulled her to him. "Does that feel like I don't want you?"

It didn't. It felt like there was a baseball bat between them.

"I've been hard for you since I turned and saw your sad little eyes. Now, no more doubts. No more tears. Only pleasure."

Alex had gone all out. There was lobster with butter sauce, asparagus, rice pilaf and double chocolate mousse. "I can't believe you did all of this. You are very talented."

"Wait until you see what I can do in the bedroom."

She didn't doubt him for a minute.

They didn't go far. He drove her to the Lost Maples National Park, just a few miles. "Tomorrow, we'll explore, take in the leaves. But tonight, the only thing that I want to explore is you."

He fed her. She had never giggled so much in her life. Butter would drip from the succulent pieces of shell fish and he would capture it with his tongue, straight off of her lips. The mousse proved to be not only a culinary adventure, but an erotic one. This time she got in on the act, sitting astraddle his lap, feeding him spoonful after spoonful of the luscious chocolate.

Standing, he caught her by the hand. "Enough. I can't wait any longer. I'm so turned-on I ache. Come with me." He led her to the fireplace. "We're going to make out here. Afterwards, I'll take you to bed." The fire crackled and the flames danced and Scarlet's blood pressure raced madly. This incredible dream of a man was about to make love to her.

Please God, don't let me disappoint him.

They had dressed up for each other. He wore all black, black slacks, black dress shirt, no tie, but with that golden hair, he was a walking dream. She didn't have any real finery, but what she had, she wore well. It felt like silk, but it wasn't, a full red tiered skirt and a long-sleeve red peasant blouse. Not overtly sexy, but it clung in all the right places, making Scarlet feel like a wanton, exotic Gypsy. Her hair was down, just like he had said he like it, and when he laid her down on the rug in front of the warm fire, she thought she would pass out from sheer happiness.

"You don't have a bra on. I gotta tell you, the sight of your aroused little nipples tortured me all during the meal. Now that I'm almost ready to touch them, my fingers are tingling with anticipation."

"That's a spot we should probably skip." Alex

stretched out next to her and they lay face to face.

He pushed her hair over her shoulders and looked deep into her eyes. "I don't like to skip anything. I'm much too thorough." His fingertips began reading her face as if the secrets of the universe were written there in Braille. Light, soft, gentle touches. "You are so beautiful. I'll never get tired of looking at your face."

Before she could stop them, tears welled up in her eyes, his words touched her heart in ways she had never conceived. "What's this?" He kissed the tears away. "No, no, babe. No crying, not tonight."

"You are so sweet, Alex. So sweet, to do this for me. I'll never be able to repay you."

Her voice caught on the tears, cracking just enough so he had to know how close she was to crying. "Sorry, I don't mean to fall apart."

"Baby, I want you to come apart, but not from tears—I want you to fly apart in rapture. Honey, this is for you. I can't deny that. But not *just* for you." He took her bottom lip between his teeth, nibbled on it and then sucked it into his mouth, laving it with his tongue. Her top lip got the same attention, and by the time he was finished, she was kissing every part of his mouth that she could. Little whimpers of need bubbled up from her throat and he captured each one reverently, his tongue mating with hers in a dance of desire. "This is for *me*, sweetheart. I want you so much. Put your hand down between us and feel my hunger for you."

He didn't have to ask twice. Unladylike it might be, but she had dreamed of touching his manhood. There were two layers of cloth between her hands and his cock, but the cotton and the linen could not mask either the size, or the heat of the beast that she grasped. He was longer than the length of her palm, a lot longer. And over half as wide. How she would ever be able to take him inside of her was a mystery, but one she was anxious to delve into. She let her palm make itself at home on the steel-hard ridge, riding a little up and down it as she held her breath with excitement. "Does that feel like I'm an unwilling participant?" He pushed himself into her hand, moaning his encouragement at her first forays into pleasuring him.

"Can I mark you, baby? Somewhere, that only my eyes will see?" He asked this as he trailed hot, wet kisses down her throat. She nodded her assent, words beyond her ability at the moment. Pulling the ties that held the neck of her blouse in place, he loosened them, pushing her top off of her shoulders. The soft skin of her neck, shoulders and upper chest were exposed for his viewing pleasure. "Right here." He touched the soft swell of her upper breast. "Can I mark you here?"

"Yes, please," she begged. She felt his teeth and lips caress an area so close to her areola that she trembled with need. The sweet suction that he applied to her flesh caused her womb to contract. "Let's take off your blouse, doll."

Alex eased the blouse on down, but she caught it with both hands, holding the material in place over her breasts. "They're too small, you're going to be disappointed," she whispered almost shamefully.

"Oh, Scarlet, my love. I know exactly how big your breasts are, and their shape. I've undressed you with my eyes every time I look at you. The first day you were here, I couldn't take my eyes off that little pink camisole you were wearing. Every time you turned a certain way, I got a glimpse of the sweetest pink nipples I have ever had the pleasure to see. I can't wait to see you naked, I'm literally trembling with the need to caress your breasts." There was a lamp on in the corner of the room, but he could clearly see her face in the firelight. Slowly, she removed her hands so Alex could lower her shirt. She closed her eyes, dreading to see the look on his face when he first beheld their diminutive size.

She couldn't see him, but she could hear him. She heard a harsh intake of breath and then a low, appreciative groan. "Dear God, baby. You're perfect." Scarlet felt his hands cover her, molding and shaping her breasts in the palms of his hands. Unbelievable sensations began to build, she had no idea the joy that could be experienced from a man's simple touch. "Open your eyes, baby, watch me worship you."

Slowly, she did as he asked. The extreme pleasure she was feeling seemed to slow time to a crawl. What she saw took her breath away. His expression was so intense, his eyes so loving. It was apparent that he was experiencing as much excitement from touching her as she was from being touched. An unexpected groan escaped her lips as he pulled on her nipples, milking them, rolling them between his fingers.

"Alex, honey, that feels…" Scarlet cried out as bliss washed over her. When Alex took one of her nipples into his mouth and began to suckle, she nearly fainted from the pleasure. The sight of him as he feasted at her breast turned her world upside down.

He tongued her, swirling around her ultra-sensitive tips. He laved her, providing just enough friction to cause her hips to buck. When he opened his mouth wide enough to swallow her whole—she thought she would die. "Alex…something's happening, love. No, I don't want it to be over so soon."

Her back arched off the floor, pushing her breasts farther into his face. He sucked hard, grunting his excitement with every pull. He felt her muscles tense and knew she was close to an orgasm. Pulling back, he led her to rapture. "This is just the beginning, baby. We've got all night. Let go, love. Let go. I'll catch you," he whispered to her tenderly. He placed one hand between her legs. One touch was all it took and she shattered into a million shards of light. Cries of unexpected delight filled the room. Alex held her close until she stopped quivering. Then, she shocked him.

Scarlet pushed on his shoulders, until he lay flat. Rolling over on top of him, she framed his face, fisted her hands in those fat, golden curls and began to rain kisses all over his face. "Thank you. Thank you. Thank you. That was more wonderful than I ever imagined." Placing her hand on the massive evidence of his need, she looked him straight in the eye and asked in a sultry little voice. "Now, what can I do for you?"

CHAPTER FOUR

"What can you do for me?" he repeated her question. Standing, he pulled her to her feet. "You can go to bed with me. You can let me love you all night long. That's what you can do for me." He led her to the master bedroom. The room, while large, was almost completely dominated by the massive bed. Candles were lit, and Alex had strewn rose petals all over the black satin sheets.

"Alex, this is…" Scarlet stopped talking. She hung her head for a moment, seeking composure. "I never expected anything like this, not in a million years. You're so good to me."

"Baby, you're easy to be good to." He began to unzip her skirt. "Let's get you out of the rest of these clothes." She followed his lead and began to unbutton his shirt, and then unzipped his pants.

Looking up into his eyes, she took his breath away. "This is going to be wonderful isn't it?"

"Yes, baby, it is." Naked, he stretched out on the bed, pulling her down with him. "I know you're ready for me, but I'm going to feel, just to be sure. Okay?" She lay beside him, completely trusting. He parted her legs, then slipped his hand over her tender pussy. She was hot and wet, as eager for him as he was for her. "Scarlet, you are so responsive. I can't wait to bury myself deep inside of you."

"I want you, Alex. I want you. Please, take me. Don't make me wait." She didn't have to ask twice. He began to sheathe himself with a condom. She stopped him. "I've been on the pill for years, please let me feel all of you. Just once." Putting the condom aside, he rose over her. Alex felt overwhelmed. This would be a first for him, also. He had never been inside of a woman without a condom. He felt like a virgin.

He stilled.

That's what she was.

Taking the greatest of care, he opened her labia, caressing the delicate pink folds. Scarlet shuddered in anticipation. She couldn't keep her hands still. She ran her palms over his shoulders and down his arms, lifting her hips in invitation. "I'm going to put my fingers inside you first, just to prepare you. Okay, baby?"

In answer, she opened her legs wider, giving him full and free access to her greatest treasure. Alex's hand shook as he sought to ready her for his possession. Slipping one finger inside of her, he moaned his excitement. She was like silk, warm, creamy silk. And God, she was tight. He was going to have to be so gentle with her. Need was causing his muscles to strain, every instinct demanded that he push into her, relieve his hunger, satisfy his tremendous appetite for the delectable woman in his arms.

Ever so gently, he moved his finger in and out, mimicking what his own flesh was ravenous to do. His efforts were met by little noises of appreciation, apparently, Scarlet was finding it enjoyable. He added another finger, widening her passage. She accepted that invasion just as gratefully. "You. Alex, I want you. Please."

Unable to deny either of their desires any longer, Alex settled himself between her thighs. Lifting her hips, he carefully placed his naked penis at the tender opening of her passage. She trembled in his arms. He was shaking, both in anticipation and in fear that he would cause her pain. "Please, Alex. You won't hurt me. Please." She urged him with her voice, as well as her body.

Surrendering, he pushed into her. Alex literally shook with excitement. "Scarlet, baby. Oh, God, this is

Heaven." Never had he felt such sweet, enveloping heat. It was like sinking down into rich, whipped cream. Alex hadn't known what a difference the lack of a latex barrier would make. He could feel the contact with her body in every cell of his engorged staff, the incredible sensation was stealing his breath away. Being inside of Scarlet was the most amazing sexual experience of his life.

But he wouldn't last.

It felt too good.

Alex was enraptured. The connection he felt with Scarlet was completely new. Her body was massaging his, molding, fisting, giving him pleasure unlike any he had ever known. He watched her face as she undulated under him. Unbelievable.

Her natural dew was bathing him in luxurious comfort, her channel was squeezing him, giving him mind-blowing ecstasy. He was so close. So close. There was no way he was going to last much longer, it was just too good. Not wanting to finish without her having another orgasm, he reached between them and began to play in her curls, finding her clitoris and rubbing it in gentle, concentric circles.

"Kiss, kiss, kiss," she begged. "I want to breathe your breath as I come." Her sentiments made him smile, even as he strived to remain coherent. The pleasure was unbelievable.

* * * *

Her body accepted him. She was grateful. He was so big, she'd had her doubts. But as aroused as she was, the entry had been almost painless. Almost. Scarlet felt her vagina stretch, making room for his sizeable girth. The feeling was unlike anything she could have imagined. Alex had taken her to such heights with his mouth at her breast, pleasuring her with his fingers—just being naked with him was a dream come true. She had never hoped to have this type of experience with a man. Oh, it had been on her list, but she had never counted on it, not really. Now it was happening and it was better than she had ever dreamed. Her body moved of its own accord. Muscles that she didn't even know she had, knotted in ecstasy.

"That's right, baby. Move for me. Does it feel good for you, baby?"

"Yes. Oh, yes. Alex, I never knew, I never imagined. You just don't know…"

She reached for his face, pulling it down so she could place her mouth over his. "Don't stop, Alex. It feels so good. Please, don't stop."

"Wrap your legs around my waist, love." When she did, he began to move harder, faster.

Touching her lips with his, he exploded, she could feel his orgasm—a white-hot surge of release. He bellowed his satisfaction, closing his eyes. She wanted to hold on to this feeling, the most intense moment of happiness in her life. He pushed into her one last time, grinding his pelvis into her tender vulva. It was just enough, she tensed and cried out. Holding him close, she quivered with intolerable pleasure. Her pussy fluttered around his cock, stealing her very breath. "Hold me, Alex. Hold me tight." He cradled her, rolling to one side, taking her with him. He was still buried deep within her, and she wanted him to stay that way. She was reluctant to break the most precious connection she had ever experienced.

"Scarlet. Oh, baby. That was so good. You are so sweet, so precious. You're my baby." He held his face to her, rubbing his nose against her skin. "Thank you. You have given me the most wonderful gift—you."

She snuggled into him, totally and absolutely

content. She kissed his chest, then put her arms around his neck and hugged him tight. "Alex?"

"What, love?"

"When I close my eyes, after I've taken my last breath..." His whole body tensed, seeming to rebel at the very thought. She held him tight, not letting him pull away, not until she finished what she had to say. "If there's nothing there—only blackness...it won't matter. I've been to Heaven, here in your arms, and it was paradise."

* * * *

He pushed a damp lock of hair off of her forehead. She had dropped off to sleep, still holding onto him. Alex couldn't sleep. He couldn't even close his eyes. All he could do was look at her. He was having trouble remembering his life before he saw her. It was as if he had started living the moment she walked into his life.

His mind was whirling. *Think, Alex. Think*. He had to make some phone calls, but first he had to have some basic information. There was no time to waste. Tightening his hold on Scarlet, he began to kiss her face, gently coaxing her awake.

Scarlet stretched, rubbing against him like a contented kitten. "Hey, baby. Can't you sleep?"

"I don't want to waste a moment of my time with you. I can sleep later."

"Sounds good. Me too. I can sleep when I'm dead." She was teasing, but he didn't take it that way.

He pulled her hands over her head, flattening her down with his body, yet not crushing, just enclosing. "*Stop*. Don't say that. Don't ever say that."

Her heart contracted, she hadn't meant to hurt him. "I didn't mean it, Alex. It's just something people say."

"You're not alone anymore, Scarlet. My life is

linked to yours. What you do, what you say, what happens to you affects me." He buried his face in her neck. "Who's your doctor, baby?"

"Dr. Haley. He's the GP back home."

"What's your blood type?" He held his breath.

Scarlet yawned, too drowsy to realize what he was doing. "Most common, O positive." Alex let out a tremendous breath of relief. They had the same blood type. Thank God! He knew there was more to it than that, but he didn't really understand what. He would, though. He intended to learn everything he could about kidney disease and the possibilities of a transplant. "What are you up to, sweetheart? Why all the questions?"

"Do you trust me, Scarlet?" he whispered in her ear. She didn't realize it, but their future hinged on her answer to this seemingly innocent question.

"With my life."

Exactly.

She had dropped right back off, physically sated and mentally content. Alex had taken longer, but gradually his body had relaxed enough for him to get a few hours rest. He still held her close, unwilling to turn her loose for a moment. He knew it was silly, but it felt like that if he kept his hands on her, nothing could happen to her. He could keep her safe.

About the time the sun began to rise, Alex awoke impossibly aroused. The woman who had him tied up in knots was warm and soft, right where he needed her to be, in his bed. "Wake up, sweet girl. I need you. Can I make love to you?"

He didn't have to ask twice. She opened happy eyes. "I was dreaming about you."

"What were you dreaming?" Whatever her dreams were, he intended to do everything in his power to make them all come true.

"That I would get one more chance to love you." The morning light filtered through the curtains, illuminating the look of total hunger on his face. They had slept unclothed, so there was no barrier to his hands or to his lips.

"Only *one* more chance? Not hardly." Alex cupped one pink tipped orb in his hand. He circled the delicate nipple, marveling at the creamy texture and the way it responded to his touch by pearling before his eyes. Lowering his head, he reverently took it in his mouth, drawing it up against his tongue. Scarlet moaned her enjoyment, holding his head to her breast, losing her fingers in his soft curls. He took his time, sucking and licking at first one globe and then the other. "I love kissing your breasts. Is it making you hot, are you ready for me, love?"

"So ready," she whispered as he angled himself over her body, supporting himself on his knees and forearms as he separated her legs and sank between them.

"Scarlet, I plan on making love to you tonight, and every night that we're together. And every morning, and every afternoon." He couldn't wait to push his aching cock deep inside of her. Nothing in his experience had ever prepared him for sex with Scarlet Rose. It was completely new. He couldn't even recall making love to any other woman, she was his first. After Scarlet, the rest of them didn't even count.

Steadying himself, he watched her face as he entered her. With a jolt, he realized that he was forever changed. The pillow on his bed would never be the same. From now on, it would be the place where she laid her head. This room would always be where he had first made love to Scarlet. Nothing would ever be as it was before. Humbled, he watched her close her eyes in ecstasy. He thanked God that his loving felt as good to her as it did to him. He watched the flush rise on her cheeks, her mouth part and that sweet pink tongue peek out and touch the bow of her upper lip.

"Alex, put him in all the way. All the way." Trembling with pleasure, she squeezed down on his shaft. It felt so good, she did it again. "I can't be still. Oh, Alex. It feels better this morning than it did last night."

Pumping into her, Alex couldn't hold himself back. Sitting up, he pulled her hips up and entwined her legs around his waist. "No, this won't be the last time we make love, Scarlet. This is just the beginning, love. Not the end." They loved each other until the last vestiges of pleasure had been drained from their bodies. Then, they lay together, lost in a dream of whispered promises and fragile tomorrows.

The day dawned bright with possibilities, they walked in the park, Scarlet couldn't get enough of just looking. The colors of the maples were truly magnificent. She and Alex walked hand in hand during the dawn's early chill. Squirrels scurried in the leaves and a hawk winged its way through the overcast sky. "I know we have to go back. But I'll never forget this time, Alex. It was absolutely perfect. You're perfect." She turned into him, fitting her body up against his. She felt confident with him, knowing that he had enjoyed her touch as much as she enjoyed his. It had made all the difference in the world.

"The first of many good times, Scarlet." She didn't answer him, and that tore a hole in his heart. He had made her happy. The next thing he had to do was give her hope.

* * * *

Cecile arrived. She was a pretty, vivacious ball of

energy. She hadn't been there ten minutes before she had Annalise and Scarlet both in stitches. Scarlet had never met her before, but she had heard so much about her, it didn't take long for them to form a bond. "So the two older brothers have been claimed." Cecile sighed. "That's a shame."

Scarlet protested, "I have no claim on Alex." Not that she didn't wish it with her whole heart, but it simply wasn't true.

"Yeah, right." Her sister winked.

Cecile was as cute as a bug, the kind of a woman that men liked to look at. She was curvy and flirty, curly dark hair that hung to her shoulders and eyes that were as green as the emerald isle itself.

"There *is* another brother." Annalise smiled wickedly. "Tall, dark, handsome. Body to die for. A football player."

"Bobby. Sweet, gentle Bobby." Scarlet summed up.

"Sounds dreamy." Cecile agreed. "The only problem is that he's what, twenty-one?"

"Twenty-two, he's a senior at UT."

"Yeah, a senior." Cecile laughed. "And I, comparatively speaking, am a Senior citizen."

"Nonsense." Annalise waved her hand. "You're gorgeous and so is he, a perfect match."

"We'll see. Now, where is that dress I've been hearing so much about?" Cecile headed toward Annalise's room.

Scarlet worked for a half hour, pinning and perfecting.

"This looks great on you." Annalise complimented her friend. "You two are going to be the most beautiful attendants that a bride could want." Scarlet's hand stilled.

"Attendants, plural?" She looked at her sister like she had grown two heads. "Cecile is your maid of honor,

79

she is your only attendant."

"No." Annalise emphasized. "Cecile is my bridesmaid. *You* are my maid of honor."

"No. I'm singing at the wedding." Scarlet was panicking.

"Yes. My maid of honor is singing at my wedding," the bride insisted. "You're scaring me Scarlet. What are you getting at?"

Scarlet quickly covered. "Nothing. Nothing. Just giving you a hard time." *Shit*!

Scarlet picked up her scissors and pins. "Slip off the dress, Cecile and I'll have it finished in no time." What in the world was she going to do? Leaving her sister and her agent to catch up, Scarlet escaped to her room.

* * * *

Alex had been busy. He had spent the day at the library, learning everything he could about antigens and antibodies. Now, he knew that just being the same blood type was just the first hurdle in being approved as a viable kidney donor. Next, he would talk to his doctor. Right now, he was going home.

To Scarlet.

When he arrived, he found her in her room. She was scrambling through her box of sewing scraps, holding up the larger pieces, laying them on the bed, then picking them up and starting over.

He went to her, picked her up and swung her up in his arms. "How's my baby?" She never questioned his affection, she just returned it tenfold.

Hugging him tight in return, she whispered in his ear. "Not too good."

Immediately, he sat her down and ran his hands over her. "Where does it hurt?"

Realizing that she had scared him, she sought to put

him at ease. "No, Alex. I've messed up Annalise's wedding."

"You've saved Annalise's wedding. What are you talking about?" She went back to examining the larger pieces of pink material.

"I need to make another dress." Turning to him, she wearily laid her head on his chest. "I thought that Cecile was Annalise's *only* attendant."

Alex let a low laugh rumble out. "Let me guess. You're supposed to be an attendant." When she nodded, he laughed louder. "Now, how did you misunderstand that? Didn't it occur to you that you would be her maid of honor?"

"She never said. She asked me to sing, that's all." He hugged her tight. "Even when we talked about the dress, she never made it clear."

"Can you do it? Do you have time?" She turned around to face the bed again and Alex kneaded her shoulder muscles, offering his support.

"I could. It's just there's so little material." She laid one piece next to the other. "If I made a straight sheathe…"

Dizziness forced her to sit down. Alex knelt at her feet. "What do you need? How about one of your pills?"

"No," she dismissed his question just a little too quickly. Picking up the material, she hunted for a pair of scissors. Alex walked to the bathroom, Scarlet tried to stop him.

"Alex, wait."

He ignored her. Going to the vanity, he picked up one of the medicine bottles. It was empty. He picked up another. It was empty, too. Striding back to her, he said flatly. "You've let yourself run out of medicine."

"No, I just haven't gotten around to getting it refilled yet." She avoided looking at him.

"I'll drive you to town. You can buy more

material." This was a test.

"I'll make do." She stared down at her hands.

"You don't have money for more material, do you?" He spoke gently. "You didn't get your medicine refilled because you used all of your money on the wedding dresses and the cakes."

"It's my responsibility. I am the bride's family."

"Annalise has loads of money, she could have spent her own money for the dress and the cake and never looked back. And I have money. I'll buy you anything you need." He knelt by her.

She didn't answer him. He continued reasoning, putting two and two together. "You couldn't tell her the truth without explaining why it is that even though you have two jobs, you don't have any money to spare. And let me guess, you canceled your hotel reservations for next week didn't you?" Scarlet looked at him, she wasn't mad. Running a hand through his soft hair, she simply said.

"How did you get to be so smart?"

Standing up, he directed. "Get your coat. We're going to town. Our first stop will be to get your medicine. Next, we'll buy whatever you need for the dress. Hell, let's just buy you a boutique dress and then you won't have to worry with making it."

"No," she faced him adamantly. He crossed his arms over his chest and stared her down. She mirrored his movements. This made him smile.

"Please," he changed his tactics.

"I won't take money from you."

"This is nothing. Don't you know what I'd give you if I could?" *Time in a bottle*. "Come on."

"You don't realize how much this medicine is going to cost." She hadn't moved a muscle.

"How much?"

"Over five hundred dollars. I can wait."

He walked back to the bathroom, gathered her bottles, and then took her by the hand. "No, you can't. You are too precious! Every moment is precious!"

This time when he walked, she followed.

"Sit close to me." He placed her on the custom bench seat of his H1 Hummer.

First, Alex got her prescriptions refilled. He didn't blink an eye at the price. The more he found out about Scarlet and her medical situation, the more he hated the American health care system. Pre-existing conditions. No insurance. Paying full price for over-priced drugs. It was a crime. He wanted ten minutes alone with every Congressman who fought the health care bill.

Next, they found a mall that seemed to look promising. Luckily, it had a Hancock Fabrics. Scarlet had insisted that this dress had to match the other one exactly, thereby negating his offer to buy her a ready-made dress. She had a sales clerk cut the material, while she gathered thread and a zipper. Alex waited patiently, seemingly oblivious to the open stares and gawks from the women, young and old.

After the fabric store, he led her down the center of the mall looking for a shoe store.

"I can make do. I have ballet slippers."

"No, we're going to get some pink shoes, or whatever Cecile is wearing." His stride was twice as long as hers.

"Silver. Slow down, Alex." She was doing her best to keep up. He stopped, abruptly. "Are you tired?"

"No, your legs are long. I can't keep up." It bothered him that she was breathing hard. He slowed down, chastened. He would need to be more careful with her.

They found a beautiful pair of silver pumps which cost three times more than they should have. It didn't matter to Alex. "I feel like a kept woman," she mumbled.

"Good. Because I plan on keeping you."

On the way home, Scarlet fell asleep, and he was glad. She needed all the rest she could get. When they pulled up at the B&B, he woke her with a kiss. "We're back, treasure." She bounced out and insisted on helping him unload the packages. "I'm going to help you, just decide what you'll let me do." He was dead serious.

"How would you like to be my dressmaker's dummy?" She teased him and then cracked up at the shocked look on his face.

"Watch it, Scarlet Rose! I'll paddle that sweet ass of yours."

"Promises, promises."

Oh, she was gonna get it, and he was gonna enjoy giving it to her.

Seed pearls. Seed pearls. Seed pearls. He was tired of seeing seed pearls. Finally, Scarlet had finished the bridal gown. Alex had been with her all the way. Cecile's dress had been next. It hadn't been hard to finish, a nip here a tuck there. Her own dress was a different matter. He had sat by while she worked on it for hours. Finally, he had to leave her and go to work, spending the afternoon in the field, straightening out one mess after another that Rick LeBeau had made. If he weren't so preoccupied with Scarlet, he would call LeBeau in for a pointed discussion. That evening, when he found his Scarlet, she was curled up on the floor, asleep. He picked her up and laid her on the bed, throwing an afghan over her.

"Alex," Ethan appeared out of nowhere.

"What?" Alex whispered.

"You've got company." Ethan raised his eyebrows as if he were trying to convey panic.

Who in the world? With one more look at his

Scarlet, he followed his brother out the door.

Sandy.

He had forgotten all about his off-hand invitation. She was there and she was dressed to kill. Everyone else was standing, watching, and waiting to see what he would do. None of them had really talked about his relationship with Scarlet, but he knew that Annalise was somewhat aware. "Hey, big boy." Sandy sauntered up to him and plastered herself to his front. "I'm here. Did you miss me?" She wasn't shy at all, she wrapped her arms around his neck and was just about to lay one on him, when Alex looked up. Scarlet stood in the doorway. Her eyes were big and wide. It was the same look she had given him after he had been so cruel to her the first day they met. He froze. She stood there, just a moment, before she turned and walked away. He dealt with his problem.

A few moments later, he found her. She was on the bed, her back to him, very still. Alex crawled in the bed with her, molding himself to her back, completely enclosing her in his arms. To Alex's relief, she didn't pull away. "She's gone, love. I had forgotten she was coming. The arrangements were made before you came, sweetheart."

Scarlet interrupted him, turning in his arms, facing him. "It's okay. You need to date. You can't let me stand in your way. What we have is only temporary. In a little over a week, I'll be gone…"

This time Alex interrupted her. "I don't want Sandy Moffett. I want you." He slid down her body, finding her braless breast through her shirt. Taking it in his mouth, he began to suckle, softly. In just a few seconds, he had her squirming with delight. Before she knew it, he had her out of her clothes, flat of her back and he was making himself happy between her legs.

"Alex, I've never…" Her breathing was erratic, her

ability to lay still—gone. He kissed her from knee to thigh, up one side and down the other.

"Lord, you are sweet. I can't wait to taste you." Scarlet grabbed the bottom sheet with both hands, clutching it in a death grip. His mouth and tongue began doing magical things to her private, pulsating core. He kissed her inner and outer lips, soft kisses that bespoke both desire and devotion. He licked the center of her cleft, making her hips levitate off the bed. Settling on her clitoris, he swirled it with his tongue, lifting the tiny hood. Scarlet's head flung from side to side, cooing noises slipping from her throat. When he put his lips around the little button and sucked, she purred like a kitten. And when he pushed his tongue deep within her passage, in and out, in and out, he pushed her completely over the edge. As she screamed, he quickly rose up and with a laugh, covered her mouth with his own, trying in vain to quell her passionate cries before his family heard them.

"Baby, baby," he crooned. "You liked that, didn't you?"

"Make love to me, Alex. I need you." She held him close.

"Do you want to be on top?" He longed to give her every experience that he possibly could.

"I just want you, it doesn't matter about the position." Scarlet held her arms out to him, and he arranged her astraddle of his lap, facing him.

"Now lift up," she held up her hips and he slid into the luscious, slick heart of her. Again, his breath was stolen in shock at how good it felt to be inside of her. It was like coming home after being away for a lifetime. Her sweet breasts were right there for the taking. He took such delight in her, mouth on her nipples, hands at her hips, helping her set a rhythm that would drive them both mad. She held on to his neck, locking her gaze with his. He knew what she was doing, she was memorizing every sensation, every iota, stockpiling memories that would get her through the hard days she thought lay ahead.

When the pleasure became more than they could bear, they gave in to the blinding, pulsing burst of ecstasy. Unwilling to end the moment, he picked her up and placed her on the pillow, then covered her with the soft sheet. "When I came home, you were asleep on the floor, exhausted. You're trying to do too much."

She didn't quibble. Instead, she laid her head on his shoulder and spoke from the heart. "I'm going to miss you so much."

Now was not the time to tell her of his plans, so he just let her talk. "What are you talking about, babe?"

"I'm going to miss your voice when you speak low and soft, just to me, telling me things only we can share. I'll miss your warmth, how solid and strong you are, and how safe I feel holding on to you as if nothing could ever harm me." He shut his eyes, fingers moving gently through her hair. "And I'll miss your eyes, how they're full of laugher and how hooded and passionate they get as you sink deep inside of me. But mostly, I'll miss you. Alex, I didn't know there was anybody like you in the world. I thank God that you came into my life."

He listened. And it took every ounce of restraint he possessed to not tell her he didn't intend to be apart from her long enough for her to miss him.

CHAPTER FIVE

Seven days before the wedding...

"Can I help you with those?" Bobby had driven up at the same time that Cecile was unloading her car.

"Sure, thanks." She didn't quite meet his gaze. "You're not shy are you?" He took the bag of groceries from her arms and another one from the seat of the car.

"I thought that if Scarlet could cook, at least I could go get the supplies. So, you're a senior at UT?" That came as a shock. He was so tall. And built. He made her feel small. And nervous.

"Yeah, I graduate in May." His smile was the cutest thing that she'd ever seen. "Is that a problem? I can't be much older than you."

She ignored his comment about her age. "Are you planning a career in football?" It wouldn't surprise her, he certainly had enough talent.

"Who knows? I don't know if I have what it takes or not. We'll have to see what happens. If it doesn't come to pass, I have other things I can do. I'm talented…in lots of areas." He smiled a wicked smile at her.

"I bet you are." Cecile could feel the heat rising in her face. She was blushing.

"God, you're cute when you blush."

Cecile knew this was fast getting out of hand. They were going to be paired up at the wedding. If the truth be known, she wanted to pair up with him in every way that counted.

"What other things can you do, Bobby?"

He let her walk up the steps of the B&B ahead of him. "Damn, you've got a fine ass."

She glanced back at him and he winked, her face

flamed with color. "Behave."

He didn't apologize, only laughed. "My repertoire is vast." When she gave him an exasperated look, he got serious. "I've got a job offer in Dallas at Raley and Sheridan."

"The engineering firm?" She was impressed. Doubly. She lived in Dallas.

"Yeah." He held the door for her. She smelled like Heaven. "Cecile, would you drive in to Austin with me for a steak?"

The look of surprise on her face said it all. "We need to talk about this. You don't want to go out to dinner with me. Don't you know how old I am?"

"No, not exactly. But whatever age you are, it's the perfect age. Because you're damn hot and I can't wait to make love to you. How's that for honesty?" They stood and faced one another. She swallowed hard, and mumbled something.

"So, is that a yes?"

She couldn't help it. She smiled. "It's a yes."

* * * *

"Did you know that Alex's birthday is the day after tomorrow?" Annalise whispered.

"He hasn't mentioned it." Scarlet thought as she spoke. *His birthday! How perfect!* She would get to spend his birthday with him. Her mind whirled. She wanted to give him the world, but since that wasn't possible, she would give him the next best thing. Her most prized possession—the sword.

It would be a perfect gift for Alex. It wasn't like she was going to need it, and she wanted him to have it. He would appreciate it. Walking quickly out of the room, she called her neighbor to get the valuable relic sent to *The Lost Maples* by overnight mail. And a cake, they would need a cake. She had to ask Ethan about Alex's favorite flavor of cake. And she had to hurry.

Ethan filled her in and she got busy. German Chocolate. He loved German Chocolate. Checking the pantry, she decided that she had all that she needed to make the rich, coconut-chocolate pastry. Annalise slipped up behind her. "Did you know that Bobby and Cecile are going out on a date tonight?"

Scarlet whirled around with a smile. She was happy and she wanted everybody else to be happy. She only had another week with Alex, but she planned to live a lifetime in that week, packing it as full of happiness and love as she could. He had worked this morning and she had finished her maid of honor dress. Physically, she was feeling great, probably due to the tender loving care that she was receiving at night. And the medicine that he had bought for her, it had done its job, also. "Good for them."

"What are you doing?" Annalise parked herself on a kitchen stool and looked at her beloved sister.

"I'm going to cook something for Alex, and the rest of you. A big pot of chicken and dumplings and a coconut pie." The smells that soon started wafting from the kitchen brought everyone else into the room. Including Alex. They were far from being alone, but that didn't stop him. He went right up behind her and pulled her back against him, kissing her on the neck.

"Hey, sweet doll. I missed you." Scarlet had lost her shyness, also. She turned and initiated a kiss that set off a chorus of catcalls.

"I'm glad you're back." Tenderly, she laid her head on his chest, relaxing for a few moments in his arms.

"Are you cooking again?" There was the slightest of censures in his tone.

"I am. The chicken and broth is simmering, the dumplings are rolled out and a coconut pie just came out of the oven. Sit down and talk and we'll eat soon. Right now, I've got to press the seams on both of the bridesmaid dresses." Before, he could stop her, she had the ironing board out of the kitchen closet.

No one else seemed to be the least bit concerned that Scarlet was cooking and ironing while everyone else sat on their rear watching her work. She seemed happy, so Alex let it go, for now.

"When you go home, Scarlet, I want you to see if you can get Mother to go through her attic and she if she can find my senior prom dress. Maybe you ought to go over and hunt it for me, she'll never get around to it."

"Sure. I'll do that for you." Scarlet couldn't stand the thought of going home. For going home meant leaving Alex. But that was what was going to happen. She might as well get used to it. "What are you going to do with your prom dress?"

"I was going to ask you to rework it for the neighborhood church bizarre. They are donating evening gowns to the less fortunate girls at the local Y." Annalise helped turn Cecile's dress inside out while Scarlet worked on her own.

"Okay, I can do that." After all, she would need as much busy work as she could get to make the days and nights without Alex bearable. Right now, she couldn't even bring herself to meet his gaze. She was afraid of what she might see. He might look sad to think about her being gone, worse—he might not.

"What about that dress that you made for your junior prom? I saw it once, and it was beautiful. Would you consider donating it?" Annalise asked and Scarlet lowered her head and answered.

"Actually, I planned on wearing it to your rehearsal dinner. After all, it's just like new. Remember, I didn't have it on very long." She looked at Annalise, trying to convey the message for her to change the subject.

"That's right." Annalise winced. "What was his name? That guy that stood you up? I was out of commission for most of that year, I missed a lot." When her sister said that, Scarlet mellowed. Her embarrassment over the prom fiasco was nothing compared to the pain and trauma of Annalise's rape.

"Rick LeBeau." Scarlet's quiet answer got everyone's attention.

Ethan asked. "Did you say Rick LeBeau?" He looked Alex full in the face.

"What did LeBeau do?" Alex asked, he couldn't help himself.

This wasn't something that Scarlet wanted everyone to know, especially Alex. She had no desire for him to know her shame. But the cat was out of the bag now, so if she didn't tell it, Annalise would. "Nothing, really. He asked me to the prom and then he didn't come pick me up." She didn't look up.

Alex could picture her getting ready for the date, waiting, and then realizing that no one was coming to take her to the prom. "Bastard."

Annalise connected the dots. "Alex, is this the same Rick LeBeau that works for you? You said he was from our home town."

"Yeah, apparently." Alex's voice was low and hard.

"He's the one that told you about me, wasn't he? It makes sense now. He always did get some type of odd thrill from making fun of me." Scarlet looked at Alex sadly.

"Yes." Alex's voice seemed filled with anger and shame.

"What are you talking about?" Annalise asked, unaware of all that had transpired. And Scarlet planned to keep her that way.

"Nothing, sweetie." Quickly, she veered the subject to the first thing that she could think of. "I did find out something odd about him not too long ago." She looked at her sister full in the face. "Did you happen to know that he's Jeff's half-brother?"

Annalise went pale. Ethan leaned over and touched her hand. "You don't mean Jeff Ramsey, do you?" Seeing, how her sister reacted, Scarlet was sorry she brought it up. Jeff was Annalise's first husband. If he could be called a husband. Their marriage had only lasted one day, he had been an immature bastard who was turned off by the scars she had received at the hand of her rapist. Just a few months ago, he had turned up and tried to force Annalise to give him money. He had even attempted to kill her.

Scarlet answered softly, "Yes. They have the same mother, but different fathers."

Annalise looked at Alex. "Be careful of Rick, if he's as crazy as his brother, he'll bear watching."

"Don't worry about that, I will." He couldn't imagine that he was actually dangerous, but Alex had already decided to keep an eye on him, anyway.

Scarlet was having trouble with subject changes. Time to try again. She needed to learn to keep her mouth shut. "Do you have anything else that needs ironing? Do you Ethan? Alex?" Scarlet quickly changed the subject, not wanting her sister to dwell on all the painful details. Annalise was easily distracted, heading to her room and retrieving four pieces of clothing that could use a touch up.

"I think Bobby has some shirts, too. Alex, how about you?" Annalise was still looking for garments for Scarlet to iron.

"No! No! No!" Alex shouted, standing up and walking over to Scarlet. "You've done enough. You cook for everyone. You sew. You still have to bake the cakes. You are not going to do everyone's ironing. And to make matters worse—" Scarlet realized that Alex was about to tell everyone about her illness. She stopped him. With her mouth. She kissed him long and hard. When they separated, Annalise and Ethan was nowhere to be found.

"I like the way you shut me up." Alex smiled.

"Well, I couldn't very well let you tell Annalise about my kidneys. But, mainly I kissed you because no one has ever stood up for me like that before. Nobody." She held him tight.

Annalise came back in, and without a word, went right to the ironing board. Alex kissed her on the forehead and left the two sisters to work out their differences.

"I'm sorry, Scarlet. I didn't intend to take advantage of you."

"It's okay, Alex is just over-protective."

Annalise giggled, "That was the sexiest damn thing I've ever seen. You are one lucky girl."

Scarlet finished up the chicken and dumplings and listened as her sister shared what her next romance novel was going to be like.

* * * *

Alex walked off his angst. He was so angry. At himself. At Rick. At life. Ethan joined him.

"So, that's how it is, huh?"

"Yeah, that's how it is," he said gruffly. "I love her, Ethan. Completely. Irrevocably."

"Does she know?"

"No. I mean, we haven't said the words."

"What are you waiting for, brother?"

"She's sick."

Ethan stopped in his tracks. "What did you say?"

"She has kidney failure. She's had it since the operation on her foot. Time has run out for her. She's either going to need dialysis or a transplant and it doesn't look like she will get either. She has no health insurance."

"What about…" Ethan couldn't bring himself to say it.

"Neither Annalise nor her mother have the right blood type. Her dad did, but he's dead." Alex could see the relief in his brother's eyes. He didn't like it, but he understood it. "I'm compatible, I don't know if I'm suitable for a transplant, but my blood type is right and I'm going to get the rest of it checked out. Soon."

"Wow. I don't know what to say." Ethan was stunned.

"She has a problem with taking a kidney from a living donor. We've got to work that out." Alex was talking fast now. He was so desperate to help Scarlet that it was physically getting to him. He wanted to bellow in frustration. He wanted to hit something.

"How?"

"I'm going to marry her."

"What?"

"I don't know how I'm going to convince her or what I'm going to do. She's not going to go along with it, she has this stupid idea that she would be a burden. And she never wants to be a burden to anyone."

Alex looked so sad, that Ethan racked his brain for an answer. Suddenly, he had an idea. A crazy idea. "Alex, marry her at the wedding rehearsal. You'll be standing up for me and Scarlet will be standing up for Annalise. You can get a special license, marry her, then, when you have her bound to you for life, you can convince her it's a good idea."

"What you said started out sounding like a good idea, but the longer you talked, the scarier it got." Alex was actually laughing. Ethan had accomplished his goal.

"I'm really not kidding." Ethan was serious.

"I know." Alex was deep in thought. "And that's why I'm going to do it." He put his arm around his brother. "I need for you to pull in every favor you can. Here's what I've got to have…"

* * * *

"Can you imagine how happy Annalise and Ethan are going to be?" Scarlet held herself around the waist and twirled around. "Just imagine. Getting to marry the one you love."

As she said the words, she looked at him intently. The one he loved was standing right in front of him. "I can imagine," Alex said quietly. "Come here to me, Scarlet." He held out his hand.

Without a moment's hesitation she went to him. He began to slip her dress over her head. She let him do what he wished with her. When her arms were free, she unbuttoned his shirt, pushing it from his shoulders. "Alex, will you teach me how to please you?" She reached out and placed her hand over his already engorged cock.

He let out a half laugh, half gasped as the reality of what she was asking sank in. "Baby, anything you do excites the hell out of me."

"Show me how to touch you," she insisted. Unzipping his pants, she urged him to completely undress. He sat on the edge of the bed and she settled herself between his legs. Alex hesitated. He wasn't shy, but the mental image of Scarlet pleasuring him was paralyzing. "Show, me Alex. I want to know." She looked up at him with such sweet sincerity, that he could deny her nothing.

He stroked himself a few times, then stopped. "Scarlet, it's your touch that sends my blood pressure through the roof." She took him at his word, and replaced his hand with her own, moving it up and down his shaft, the way that he had done. He leaned back, closing his eyes, enjoying her touch. In a few moments, a new sensation was added, one that felt like the brush of an angel's wing. Unable to deny himself the sight, he watched as she swirled her soft pink tongue around the head of his penis. Taking the initiative, her other hand cupped his balls, massaging and cupping, completely eradicating the air from his lungs. "Is this good?"

"God, yes," he groaned.

"How far should I take him in my mouth?"

"Only as far as is comfortable for you," he was struggling to talk. "I have to lie down." Alex collapsed backwards, unable to think or breathe.

With finesse she shouldn't have had, she brought him to a raging climax, loving him until he was completely drained, making his toes curl with the kind of satisfaction that he had rarely achieved in any sexual experience. Except with Scarlet.

"Baby, I have to ask. I know that up until a few days ago, you were an innocent. How did you do that? How did you know what to do?" His voice and tone was one of awe and amazement.

She rose up, propped her chin on his middle and answered him primly. "Alex. Why are you surprised? After all, I am a librarian."

He laughed. "You are a mess and a half." He grew serious. "Now, tell me what you have against accepting a kidney from a living donor?" He had covered her with a quilt, holding her close. Just as soon as he regained his strength, he planned on loving her till she screamed, but right now he needed to understand.

"My friend Angie was sick and needed a kidney, her brother donated one of his. He died on the operating table. She lived, he didn't, it haunts me to this day." Turning to face him, she pressed her face to his chest, listening to his heartbeat. "I could never put anyone I loved in jeopardy like that. Not for me. I would rather die any day, than risk the life of someone I loved. It's just not worth it." She kissed him on his collar bone, loving the feel of his hard muscles against her cheek.

"You do realize how rare that is. Ninety-nine point nine percent of the people who donate their kidneys make it through the operation just fine. And they go on to live full and active lives." As he talked, he felt Scarlet draw back. He pulled her up against him, even closer. "Don't you know how precious you are?"

"Alex, I told you that I don't have anyone to ask. Besides, do you know how much a kidney transplant would cost?"

"How much?" He knew, but he wanted to see what she would say.

"Three hundred thousand dollars," she said flatly. "It might as well be three hundred million dollars. I don't have any way of getting that kind of money."

"Annalise is a writer, a successful author. She has that kind of money." He had no intention of Annalise paying for Scarlet's operation, but he was testing the waters.

"Alex." Scarlet propped herself up on him, completely oblivious to the way her plump little breasts looked pooled on his chest. "When I was growing up, I had to accept help from people. I was clumsy and awkward. I couldn't carry anything or open doors for myself. For sixteen years, I was a burden to my family." He started to speak, but she put a hand over his mouth. "I will never be a burden to anyone I love. Ever again. No. I can't ask Annalise for anything. I don't want her to even know that I have a problem. I want this week to be perfect, it will probably be the last time that I see her. Please."

Alex's heart felt as if it would break in two. "You're

wrong, baby. So wrong." He wanted to tell her that there was no way he was going to let anything happen to her, but now was not the time. She was in no mood to listen to reason. So he comforted her in the only way that she would allow. He made love to her.

Lord, in heaven. She was like a fever in his blood, the taste of her kiss, the feel of her skin, the way that she whimpered so sweetly when he entered her body—all of this combined to bring him to the point of obsession. "Turn over, precious." She was always ready for him, he didn't even have to ask. Eager to please him, she turned her bottom up and made him welcome. He fitted himself to her, into her, pistoning home with each stroke of his body. Leaning over, he clasped her sweet breasts, causing her to moan at the caress of his hands. "You're a fever in my blood, Scarlet." He kissed her on the shoulder. "I have Scarlet Fever." His words seemed to set her on fire, she pushed back against him, wanting to feel every inch, every thrust. "Come up here, love." He pulled her up and back against him, so that her back was against his front.

"Touch me here, please." She guided his hand to her mons, eager for him to stroke her clit. He swirled and petted her pearl of passion, causing her to writhe in ecstasy.

He watched her come apart in his arms, her hand reaching behind his head to pull his lips down to hers. Alex didn't last but a stroke or two longer, the pleasure was just too intense. He held on to her though, not letting her separate from him.

* * * *

Scarlet wasn't trying to get away. She was doing her best to absorb every sensation, every touch, every kiss so she could replay it later like a precious recording of a blessed event. Laying her head back against him, she spoke before she thought. "I love you." The words had no more left her mouth, before she realized what she'd said. What had she done? Tearing herself from his embrace, she grabbed her robe. "I didn't mean to say it, Alex. I'm sorry." He tried to grab her hand, to stop her.

"Scarlet, wait!" Refusing to look at him, she fled the room. It was late enough that everyone else was in their rooms, she wouldn't have to explain. Blindly seeking the door, she ran from the inn, seeking the cover of darkness. Tears were streaming down her face, adding to her inability to see where she was going. Dashing them away with her hand, she glanced back, hoping that Alex wouldn't follow her. What would she say? They had no future, she had no right to say those words to this wonderful man. Running to the back of the main house, she headed for the grove of trees that grew along the side of the rushing stream. The sound of the water hid the approaching footsteps, and Scarlet did not know Alex had followed her until he swept her up in his arms.

"Don't ever run away from me, Scarlet. Run to me. Always. Run to me." He cradled her against him, placing kisses all along her hairline and across her eyelids. "I love you, baby. I love you more than you could ever know. We are going to work this out. Trust me, Scarlet. I will make all this okay for you."

Holding on to him, she wanted to believe his words more than anything. "I wish you could. But you can't." She put a small hand to his cheek. "And it's all right, Alex. It's all right."

"I love you, Scarlet." He said it again, just in case she missed it the first time.

"And I love you, Alex." He let her slide down his body, so that he could envelop her in his arms, kissing her passionately.

"You are mine. You belong to me. I will take care of you." Scarlet let his words nourish her soul. He meant them. He really meant them. That it didn't matter in the long run was of no consequence. They might not have forever, but they had the here and now. And the here and now was the sweetest place that Scarlet had ever been.

* * * *

"I want to make love to you, Cecile." Bobby caught her hand, pulling her toward the bed.

Cecile looked at the broad shoulders and perfect abs of the young Adonis that lay across her quilt. "I want to. I really do. Actually, I'm shivering just thinking about what you might look like under those jeans, but I can't."

"Why?" Bobby rose from the bed and slowly began to stalk her. "I've been hard for you for two days, lady. I don't think I can wait any longer." She backed up as far as she could go, until she was leaning against the wall.

"You're very aggressive." She smiled, nervously. "I like that." She did, it made her forget their age difference. He moved directly in front of her. His broad, well-developed chest was close enough that her aroused nipples almost brushed against him.

"I know what I want, and I go after it." He bracketed her with his arms, leaning in, perilously close to her lips. "And I want you, Cecile. In my bed. Now."

"I was in elementary school when you were born," she muttered weakly.

"So? I think I've caught up with you, darling." He inhaled her scent, his lips making a foray down the soft skin of her neck.

"I was in college when you were in Junior High." Her voice was even weaker, the argument not even standing up in her own mind. Not anymore. This youngest Stewart brother was sexy as hell.

"You are the cutest, sweetest, softest, sexiest woman that I know. I'm going to kiss you now, if you're through worrying about our school days." Cecile opened her mouth to say something else, but she couldn't think of anything to say. Her eyes were focused on his full, chiseled mouth, the lower lip a little fuller than the top lip. There was a cleft in his chin and a dimple to the right of his mouth. Bobby took advantage of Cecile's parted lips. He covered her mouth with his, letting his tongue tease hers into submission.

"That's right, doll. Kiss me. Kiss me, hard." With a whimper, Cecile surrendered. She pushed off the wall and into his arms, her hands cupping his head. He cupped her butt and picked her up, her legs parted and made themselves at home around his waist. "Oh, yeah. I can feel how hot you are, right through your jeans." His words excited her so, that she pressed herself against him.

"Oh, Bobby," she moaned. "I need you."

"You got me, baby. All night long."

* * * *

Six days before the wedding . . . . .

Scarlet taught them all how to play marbles. Not the 'get down and shoot marbles out of a circle' type game, but the board game that was played with a deck of cards on a specially designed game board. It was a vicious game, and Scarlet was good at it. She explained the rules of the game, how you could help your partner or take out your enemy. Partnering with Alex, he saw a side of her that he had not known existed. She was ruthless. Except with him. She played hard and laughed harder. He was totally fascinated by the sheer joy she pulled from every moment.

She took him ghost hunting. They had to use his camera, but he had a blast. They waited until almost midnight before heading to the old country cemetery just down the road. The graveyard was enclosed by a hurricane fence and the gate creaked ominously as they opened it. He couldn't help but smile as she addressed the occupants and asked their permission to come in and visit. "I have a theory, you know."

"You do? Tell me about it." He didn't know whether he wanted to hear this or not.

"I've seen many things through the lens of my camera. Everything from full body apparitions to clouds of ectoplasm, but the most common form that I see is a ball of energy. They come in every color in the rainbow and every size imaginable. One minute you'll be alone and the next you'll be surrounded by a million of these orbs. They seemed to respond to my voice." As she talked, she turned on the camera and began to take pictures. Leaning over, she showed him what she had captured on the digital image. Alex caught his breath. He didn't know what he had expected, but it wasn't this. There were beautiful balls of light in the photographs. They were not clear or white, but a shimmering opalescent color that contained every hue of the rainbow.

"They're beautiful." He kept his voice low, out of respect, he guessed.

"Back to my theory. I think that this may be the form in which the soul travels. In my studies, I've discovered that reported sightings of ghosts normally occur in places that the person visited in real life. They are never seen where they have never been." Alex looked at her, trying to understand what she was getting at.

"Now, that I've been here, with you—I can come

back." He closed his eyes as a wave of sorrow hit him. She was talking about dying.

"So you think the soul of a person can return to every place that he has visited?"

"Yes, especially if the place is important to them or the people that live there are important to them." Unable to restrain himself, he carefully took the camera from her hands and sat in on a nearby bench. Then, he picked her up and held her like he would never let her go.

After they had returned from the cemetery, Alex had been subdued. But Scarlet was having none of it. She had given up all pretense of sleeping in her own room and had moved openly into Alex's. "I just need to hold you." Alex had tried to force Scarlet to rest.

"No, baby." She had practically begged. "I only have a few more nights to spend in your arms. I can't afford to waste a moment." Her sweet pleas had melted his heart and his reservations.

"A lifetime, Scarlet. We have a lifetime." He spoke the words prayerfully, as he joined their bodies in the age-old way of man and woman. As she sighed her relief, she let his words sink in. He was right. They had a lifetime. It was just a shame that it was limited to her few pitiful days.

* * * *

Five days before the wedding . . . . .

Alex's birthday dawned bright and clear. The sword had been delivered by Federal Express the afternoon before and Scarlet had to enlist Annalise's help to hide it until Scarlet could wrap it. Her sister had not fully understood how she could part with her most valuable possession. The truth was, the sword didn't come close to be her most valuable possession, Alex was. Or rather the way she felt about him. The love she had for Alex was worth more to her than all the gold in the world. Its value lay in its rarity, the surprise of it, and the unexpectedness. She had never hoped or dreamed to find love in her short life, yet here it was. Her treasure.

While Alex was gone to call on some clients, Scarlet made his birthday cake and wrapped the sword in one of the boxes she had used to transport Annalise's wedding gown. That way, the identity of the present was securely hidden. He would never guess what was in the box. Lovingly, Scarlet iced the cake, and then wrapped the gift. This would be the only birthday she would share with him and she wanted him to remember it. And remember her. Scarlet had thought of that a few times, being remembered. Before, her life remembrances had lain in the hands of her sister and the children with which she worked. Now, she would live on in Alex's memory.

* * * *

The meeting was not going well. Alex was giving LeBeau enough rope to hang himself with and the walk to the gallows was going to be a short one. "So, tell me about the church mouse?"

"Scarlet was, how shall we say—unexpected." Alex was careful not to give away how he felt about her. He was intending to let LeBeau have his say and then he would have his.

"Yeah, unexpectedly homely." Rick laughed, reaching in his pocket and making sure the digital recorder was turned on.

"I understand that you asked her to the prom?" Alex had to hold on to the desk to keep from lunging at the puke.

"Now, that was hilarious. Who told you about that? I played along with her for weeks, even held her hand a few times. She planned and planned, the color of her dress, if I was going to buy her a corsage, where we would go to eat. I think she made herself a dress and I was to wear a matching cummerbund. My only regret was not getting to see her face when she finally realized that I had stood her up. Classic, man. And did they tell you what I did to her at Senior Trip?"

"No, tell me." Alex managed to say.

"We were scheduled to leave at eight that morning. I had some of the guys tell her eight-thirty, just so she'd arrive as the bus was leaving. She couldn't run, you know. It was priceless." Rick shook his head, as if the recollections were so good they were meant to be relished.

"Rick, I need to tell you something."

"Yes, boss?"

"You're fired." Sweet words.

"Why?" Rick couldn't believe it.

"To start with, you do a piss-poor job. But I could have trained you, shaped you into a better employee. What I can't shape you into is a decent person. Scarlet is the most wonderful woman on the face of the Earth. She is beautiful, kind, smart and I love her with all my heart. I'm going to marry her at the first opportunity. And the one thing I don't need around is you. You've caused her pain. Needless, stupid pain. And if I do anything in my life that is at all worthwhile, it will be to see that Scarlet never experiences the likes of you, or anyone like you, ever again. Now, get the hell out of my office and off my property. And I never want to see your ugly face again."

"Not so fast, Stewart. I'm onto you. I know your game. You're feeling guilty about the church mouse because you're really in love with her sister. You're smitten by your own brother's fiancé. The Jezebel. She writes that porn-shit. I know all about it. My brother is in jail because of her. Now, you've fallen into her trap. And you're covering by paying attention to her homely, crippled sister." These words were said with such venom, that Alex was momentarily thrown off guard.

But not for long. Alex clenched his fist, biting his jaw to keep from striking the putrid piece of refuse that stood in front of him. "You think that I don't love Scarlet. You think that I don't want to marry her. You think that I'm in love with Annalise. Well, I think you're an asshole. I love Scarlet more than I love life itself. And you, you sniveling little bastard, are just a wart on the backside of humanity." With that, Alex grabbed Rick by the collar and shoved him through the door.

Alex sighed. That had felt damn good.

* * * *

Scarlet had coerced her sister and Ethan, along with Bobby and Cecile into going into Austin for dinner. She wanted to be alone with Alex. The cake was ready and the present was wrapped and she had cooked a huge pot of seafood gumbo. She hoped he liked it. The cake and the present were put up, she wanted it to be a complete surprise.

Annalise had let her borrow a dress that she swore Alex had not seen. It was cut so that the differences in their bust lines wouldn't be a factor in how the dress hung. It was a straight, black, backless sheathe that was shorter than anything Scarlet had ever worn before. The pumps were at least three inches and she wore a garter belt and black hose. Her hair was caught up in one of the ornate clips that she had made. She hoped it made her a little bit sexy, because Scarlet felt wanton. She hoped Alex liked the way she looked.

He did. Alex had slipped in the back way, hoping to steal a kiss before he had to make nice in front of the rest of the family. He stood in the kitchen door and felt his jaw drop. There was no doubt in his mind that Scarlet was beautiful. She had a rare elegance about her that made a man want to care for her and defend her against the world. But tonight! Tonight, she was a vixen, a temptation, a vision of lust and sinful sensuousness. He stood, weak in the knees and swollen with need.

He didn't have to move. She saw him. The look of utter joy on her face was breathtaking. "Alex!" She ran to him and he caught her. Five more days. What if he couldn't convince her to stay? Five more days. How would he ever be able to go on without her? "Happy Birthday Sweetheart!"

"Birthday? Who's having a birthday?" For a moment, she looked taken aback and then she saw the glint of humor in his eyes. "You." She kissed him soundly. "I cooked you gumbo, I hope you like it."

"Everything that you fix is out of this world." He sat down on a dining table chair and pulled her onto his lap. "You look gorgeous! Sexy as hell, let's skip dinner and go straight to the loving." He nipped at her neck and fondled her breast. In just a moment, he had her panting. She was always so in tune with his needs, Alex bowed his head against hers and cherished the moment.

"Let's eat and then I have a surprise for you."

"Is my surprise under this dress?" He ran his hand under her skirt, but she stopped him.

"You'll just have to wait and see. Besides, I have to be careful. Everything I have on is borrowed."

"I adore your sister, but you are way sexier than she is."

Scarlet laughed. "You're not supposed to think she's sexy. She's almost your brother's wife, but thank you for saying so. No one else has ever thought I was sexy."

Alex thought of that ass LeBeau. He wanted her to know that he had taken vengeance for her. "I fired Rick LeBeau today," Alex spoke slowly.

Scarlet glanced down, as if she were remembering the mean things he had done to her. "You did that for me, didn't you?"

"Of course."

"Thank you. But, I would never want you to do anything that would hurt your company. Not for me.'

"What better reason is there than you? I love you, Scarlet."

The simple words seemed to give her both pleasure and pain. Sighing, she answered in a way he understood. Reverently, she framed his face and kissed him tenderly. "I love you, too. More than you will ever know." Then, as if shedding the weight of the world from her shoulders, she jumped up and began setting out gumbo bowls and a bottle of wine. She filled his bowl and his glass and joined him at the table. "Tell me what you need to do to finish getting ready for the wedding. I want to help."

Alex covered her soft, little hand with his own. "You have your hands full with the cakes. I've visited with the caterers and everything has been straightened out. The tents will be delivered and set up early on dress rehearsal morning. The sound system and your piano will arrive at ten that day and the caterer will have all the food and the wet bar here by five for rehearsal and then by three on D day." He had to play it cool. For him, the dress rehearsal was the most important day of the two. After all, that would be their wedding day. And hopefully, it was all coming together. He and Ethan had connections and they had pulled in favors for a special license and to get her included on Alex's insurance program. As soon as they were married, Scarlet would be completely covered for dialysis. He was still working on the transplant angle. But if there was a God in Heaven, he would make that happen, too.

"The cakes aren't going to be a problem. You can put as much of this on me as you need to. I want to help you." She was absolutely sincere and Alex loved her for it.

"We'll work together. Okay?" He noticed that she wore no jewelry of any kind. Picking up her left hand, he rubbed her ring finger, thinking of the three carat diamond that was being set just for her. He couldn't wait to give it to her.

"If you're through with your gumbo. I have another surprise." She stepped into the formal dining room and came back with a huge cake.

"German Chocolate," he said with awe. "My favorite." He let her cut him a huge piece. She set it proudly before him and watched him as he enjoyed it. Slipping off one more time, she returned with a huge box. "For me?"

"Yes," she said softly. "I hope you like it."

Knowing her financial situation, he started to protest. But the look in her eye quelled anything negative that he was about to say. With a lump in his throat as big as the state of Rhode Island, he unwrapped the package. "What in the world?" Pushing back the tissue paper he uncovered her offering. "The sword!" He didn't know what to say.

"I wanted you to have it. I knew that you would appreciate it and protect it." He pulled it out and ran his hand over the ornate hilt and carefully down the long blade.

"I will cherish it, sweetheart.' He laid it down and pulled her close. "But I will cherish you more." He knew exactly what she was doing. She had bequeathed him the sword. He would accept it, but he planned to simply take care of it for her. The same way he planned on taking care of her.

CHAPTER SIX

Cecile had never known that she was multi-orgasmic. She never had been before. But with this young stud, who plowed into her like he was breaking up a fertile field, she came over and over again.

"Do I satisfy you, my lady?"

Cecile panted, laughing with what little breath she had left. "You know you do, Boy Wonder."

"Hey, if you're going to make superhero analogies, I would much rather be Superman or even the Caped Crusader." Bobby hooked a hand around her waist and pulled her close to him.

"Oh, Bobby," she sighed leaning her head over on his shoulder. "You are all of the above plus Captain America and the Juggernaut all rolled into one."

"All right! The Juggernaut! I love the Juggernaut!" Despite his bravado, Bobby tenderly tilted her face up to his lips. "You inspire me, woman. I want to make love to you twenty-four hours a day." The kiss that he placed on her lips was different from any he had bestowed upon her before. It was soft and gentle and so full of tenderness that it almost made her cry.

"Bobby, this has been wonderful. It was so unexpected, such a sweet surprise." The more they were together, the more she realized how much they had in common. They both liked jazz, hiking, reading murder mysteries, left wing politics and donating time to Habitat for Humanity.

"I don't want it to be over, doll. I'll be moving to Dallas in a few months. I want to continue seeing you.

Would you like to be my girl?" His words made her shake.

"Bobby, you are so sweet." She wanted to say yes. In fact, she wanted to scream yes. But, she was older than him.

He rolled her over, and lay on top of her, effectively trapping her beneath his large, hard body. "Say yes. You know you want to." He grinned, he wasn't crushing her, he was very careful to bear most of his weight on his knees and his arms. But he had her where he wanted her. She couldn't get away.

"I'm old enough to be..." She started talking, but then she didn't know what she was going to say. His eyes were the most incredible shade of blue.

"You're old enough to be my sweet lover. Is that what you were going to say?" He tickled her gently, absorbing her laughter into his mouth.

"Yes," she whispered. "Yes," she kissed him. "My answer is yes. I want to be your girl."

* * * *

Alex's teeth scraped and nipped the red rose on the curve of Scarlet's hip. "Scarlet Rose, you have the sweetest rear end that I have ever had the pleasure to bite." Laughter erupted from her throat and she tried to turn over, but he held her down.

"Can I ask you a question about the sword?"

"Sure, in fact, I have some documentation on it at home. I'll mail it to you as soon as I get back next week." She tried to smile, but it didn't make it to her eyes.

"That's not what I want to know." Alex turned her over, he wanted to see her face as she answered. "The sword is valuable. I did a search on it, and you could have sold it for forty to fifty thousand dollars. Why didn't you do that? You could have paid for a year's worth of dialysis treatments with that money."

Scarlet lay very still. "I hate having to explain, I don't want anyone's pity. I wish you could look at me and not think about my health problems. We only have five more days, together. Do we have to talk about this?"

"Scarlet—" he began.

"It's true that the sale of the sword would have brought enough to pay for a year's dialysis. But I still would have had to travel fifty miles, one way, every day, to take the treatments and I wouldn't have been able to work. At the most it would have only been a temporary fix. And I don't know how I would have survived without a job."

It hurt like hell, but Alex continued to push. "After the incident at the hospital, why didn't your family sue?" He was torturing her, he was torturing himself, but he needed to understand.

"Dad didn't believe in it, besides when I developed this problem after getting my club foot fixed, it just reinforced his belief that my problems were meant to be. God was in control and I was paying for my sins." Alex looked so stricken, Scarlet only sought to comfort him. "Don't you think I've explored every avenue? It's not that I want to die, Alex. I just don't have any choice. You're making this so hard, please let's just forget about it. Let's think about something else."

"You do have choices, Scarlet. I'm working on a plan to ensure that you live a long and happy life." He sat up in the bed and physically picked her up, holding her in his arms, as if he intended to never let her go.

"You are so serious, and so sweet." Scarlet rubbed his cheek. "I love you. Let's just enjoy the time we have left together, okay?"

She was asking the impossible.

* * * *

Four days before the wedding…

Alex didn't want to have to deal with this. Not now. But he had no choice, not unless he was willing to watch his business go down the drain. He walked into the kitchen, arms full of files, and sat down heavily at the table. Ethan was making coffee. "Where is everybody?"

Annalise is getting ready. We have our final counseling session with the pastor. It's required, he's adamant that we understand how serious matrimony is." Ethan looked at his brother with a smile on his face. "Like I don't realize what a big step I'm taking. The meeting is at six, so we're going to make a day of it. Maybe, even stay for dinner. Would you and Scarlet like to come with us?"

"I wish. I've got a ton of work to do. Where's Bobby?"

"Practice. Big Mack called a special session. And Cecile went with him. I think something's going on with those two. You know, it's a good thing that the Longhorns have a bye this week, or we would've had to get married on a Sunday." Ethan looked at his brother with an indulgent look on his face. "Aren't you going to ask me where Scarlet is?"

"I know where Scarlet is. I gave her a cell phone yesterday and insisted that she keep me informed if she had to leave the house."

"So, you know that she has gone to the doctor?"

"Yes, she went to the clinic to get her birth control pills refilled." Alex admitted somewhat reluctantly. "I tricked her, sort of." He rubbed a hand down his face, in worry. "Doc Gibbs wanted me to get her in there for some blood tests. He wants to know exactly where she is in her kidney function, how much time we've got to work with. So, I hid her pills. She thought she lost them." Alex looked up at his brother, with such sadness in his eyes that Ethan would have done anything for him. "Ethan, I didn't know what else to do. We needed that information. Doc Gibbs said he has to be sure there is a high probability of a tissue match. If I told Scarlet the truth, she would have flat out refused to go in at all."

"I don't blame you, I would have done the same thing for Annalise." Ethan put a comforting hand on his brother's shoulder. "On a brighter note, I got you that underhanded wedding license."

"Great news. What did you have to do, bribe the judge?" Alex wouldn't have been surprised.

"I did something really wild." Alex looked confused. "I told the truth. Raymond Lanier, the county clerk is a good guy. He understood. I told him the situation with her health and how stubborn she is, and he didn't even hesitate. He told me that he didn't think it would be a problem, that he would personally walk it by the judge. But you need to level with her at the first opportunity. Of course, if she balks on you, the judge would probably give you a quick annulment."

"Over my dead body. Once I get that ring on her finger, nothing or nobody will ever separate us again."

"Man, you're hopelessly in love. I know the feeling. What's with the pile of paperwork?"

"This is stuff that Rick left hanging. I have to come up with a proposal for a plan to power Abilene Christian with wind power, and I'm way behind. This is what I get for giving that idiot so much responsibility. I don't even have the lay-out drawn up for the wind farm."

"I wish I could help, bro." Ethan sympathized. "Unfortunately, it's not my area of expertise."

"You can help by pouring me a cup of coffee and keeping it coming." Alex bowed his head and went to work.

* * * *

Scarlet was a nervous wreck. She should have known better than to try and visit a doctor in Austin. Even if it was Alex's personal physician, he had coerced her into taking every test imaginable. There was no way all that blood work was necessary to renew her birth control medicine. But, because it was a friend of Alex's, she had gone along. He had wrote her a prescription, but told her he would be getting in touch with her later about her blood work. She left Alex's cell phone number with the nurse, who promised to call once they had the test results.

To complicate matters, she felt weaker and noticed that she was getting short of breath. It scared her to death, because she knew exactly what it meant. She was getting worse. If she could just keep it together for four more days, then she could get home and deal with it the only way she knew how.

Closing her eyes, she wondered if she would have the courage to go through with her plan. Over and over again, she had played out the scenarios in her mind. But, what haunted her the most, was getting too weak and sick to take care of herself or slipping into a coma and not being discovered until it was too late. The best solution she could come up with was to speed things along. It wouldn't take too much ibuprofen to push her over the edge. And she had already notified one of her best friends, the area funeral director. He would take care of everything else. They had bonded during the years that she had played and sang for so many funerals. Actually, he was a comfort to her, he had her back. Not a perfect solution, by any means, but the best one she had come up with. At least it gave her something to worry about besides how much she was going to miss Alex.

When she got home, she found him bent over a pile of papers in deep concentration. He didn't even hear her come in. She slipped up behind him and hugged him tight. Immediately, he pushed everything aside and pulled her around to sit on his lap. "Lord, I missed you."

Knowing that time was quickly slipping away, she sought his lips and kissed him deeply. "I missed you, too."

"Did you get your pills?"

"Yes, so we're back in business." She traced his eyebrows, burning the image of his face in her mind.

"I love monkeying with your business." Kissing the palm of her hand, he confessed. "I day dream about what I'm going to do to that lovely body once the sun goes down. But, as bad as I hate it, I have a ton of work to do."

He placed her on her feet, turned toward the files, and she pulled a chair up close to his. "Can I help?" Before he could stop her, she opened a file and looked through it quickly. "Wind farm. Do you have a topographical map? I can draw you a layout of the best grid connection possibilities and a feasibility study, if you have the wind assessment report." Alex turned completely in his chair and looked at her hard. Then he smiled the biggest, prettiest smile she had ever seen.

"God, woman, you are amazing!" He split the papers with her, anxious to see what she could do.

"Don't get too excited, yet," she cautioned him. "It's been awhile since I've had a chance to work on this type of thing. Although, I have kept up with the newest techniques and technological advances in the turbines. I'm really interested in the 'smart' turbines that the Purdue researchers have developed, the ones that can react to changing wind conditions."

"It sounds like you know exactly what you're talking about." After reviewing the reports, she went to work. He was amazed. "In a couple of hours, the project that I've been dreading, the one that should have taken me days to complete, is well on its way to being finished." Alex looked at her work. "This plan is innovative, accurate, and detailed. Your proposals make Rick LeBeau's work look like hen-scratch. Come work for me, baby. You're brilliant."

"The complement in your words makes me want to cry. No one has ever been willing to give me a chance to do what I do best, they always let my health problems define who I was and what they thought I could do, thanks. I wish I could. But I can help you while I'm here."

"I'm serious, Scarlet. I'm an employee short. You do much better work than LeBeau ever thought about doing." He watched hope fill her eyes, then it clouded over with doubt. "Think about it."

All he could think of was how awesome it would be to work alongside his wife. Alex's dreams were becoming more specific every day.

That night, Alex could tell that Scarlet didn't feel well. She had insisted that they make love, reminding him that they only had four more nights to be together. Bull! He had taken her gently, handling her as if she were made of the finest china. Breakable. Priceless.

* * * *

Three days before the wedding...

"Tell me everything." Scarlet nested down in a chair in front of the fireplace. She just couldn't seem to get warm. Alex brought her an afghan and tucked it around her shoulders.

Annalise and Cecile brought in cups of apple cider and hot chocolate for everyone. "You first, Cecile." Annalise encouraged her agent.

"Bobby took me to a great French restaurant near downtown, Aquarelle's." Nobody could miss her dreamy expression.

Scarlet leaned forward, not wanting to miss a word. "What did you have to eat?"

"We had scallops on a corn-potato compote ringed by asparagus spears. The scallops are actually cooked in truffle butter. It was the best meal that I have ever had." Cecile grabbed Bobby's hand. "Bobby ordered us a bottle of champagne. It was all very romantic."

"What did you do after dinner, did you go anywhere else?" Scarlet missed the private look that Bobby gave Cecile, but Cecile answered anyway.

"We went to a great dance club on 6th Street called Bossanova." Bobby nudged Cecile who giggled.

"How about you and Ethan, where did you go out and eat last night?" Scarlet had transferred her attention to her sister, eagerly awaiting more details.

"We went back to *our* restaurant, Selena's. It's a great Italian restaurant, built like a beautiful Tuscan villa. Ethan took me there on our first date." As Scarlet asked question after question, it hit Alex like a ton of bricks. Scarlet was trying to imagine what it was like to go out on a real date. He felt like a colossal heel. All the days that they had been together, and he had still not taken her out on the town. Watching her eyes light up as she listened to the other two women talk about where their dates had taken them and what they had eaten made Alex hurt like he'd had the wind knocked out of him.

After the conversation had died down, he eased his arm around her and pulled her close. "How about you and I go somewhere tonight? Would you like that?"

Scarlet rubbed her cheek on his shirt, and smiled up

at him sadly. "I'm really tired, love. Would you mind if we just stayed here? Or you can go, if you'd like, I wouldn't mind."

"I only want to be with you." He held her hand in his, threading their fingers together. "I'm sorry that we haven't gone anywhere like that, Scarlet. I don't know what I was thinking. I'm such an idiot."

At his words, Scarlet sat straight up and pinned him with her stare. "My time with you has been perfect. Don't you dare regret even one second of it." He closed his eyes as a lump tried to work its way up his throat. "You have shown me the time of my life, Alex. I wouldn't have missed this week with you for the world."

She was such a little firecracker. But his firecracker was fading fast. Soon, he picked her up and carried her to bed. He would let her rest for a few hours, and then he was going to turn her world upside down.

Alex called and made reservations for a dinner cruise on Lady Bird Lake. It was last minute, so he had to pay through the nose, but it was going to be worth it. Next, he called in a favor that dated all the way back to a frat-house mishap. He called Barry Ridgeway, a college buddy that had thought it was smart to invite the entire night shift of Hooters over for an after-hours soiree, complete with five kegs and the UT official canon—Old Smokey.

Alex had come home and had been shocked to find that one of the Longhorns most valuable possessions was in their back yard. Barry was so drunk he didn't realize that the whole fraternity could have been disbanded and expelled for such a stupid stunt. Alex had taken charge and returned Old Smokey, escorted the Hooters home and cleaned up Barry's mess. Barry owed him. Tonight, he would repay. Barry's family owned the South's biggest fireworks company. And the display that Alex had planned would take Scarlet's breath away.

Another favor called in, a horse drawn carriage would meet them at Zilker Park and take him and Scarlet all along the river before they boarded the dinner cruise. A call to an area florist reserved four dozen yellow roses. Alex racked his brain, trying to think of anything else he could do to make this evening perfect for her.

He had went out on a limb and paid a visit to the priciest boutique in Austin. Turning himself completely over to the sales girl, he had bought Scarlet an entire new wardrobe—including a beautiful evening gown to wear to the rehearsal dinner. There was no way he was going to let her wear a dress that she had made for another man to their wedding. He had hid everything in the far end of his closet, and now he searched through the items until he found the teal silk pantsuit he wanted her to wear tonight. Laying the items out on the bed, he added erotic matching underwear and a sexy pair of sandals. Never in a million years, did he ever consider that he would be shopping for a woman. But, truth be told, he would do anything in the world for Scarlet.

"Baby." He kissed her cheek. "I have a surprise for you, baby."

She wiggled and stretched, "I'm sorry that I slept the day away. I guess the trip to the doctor's took more out of me than I realized."

"Do you feel better?" Alex looked at her with all the love and concern that overflowed his heart.

"Yes, I do." She patted the bed. "I feel wonderful. Would you like to join me? I'll make it worth your while." Alex growled and held her down, blowing on her belly like he would a small child. Actually, her little sexy gesture had him as hard as a rock, but he had other plans. He wanted her to save all of her energy for their romantic evening. Later, he would bring her back here and give both of them what they wanted.

"Get up, baby, and put on this pretty outfit. We're going to Austin. I have a whole bunch of surprises for you."

Scarlet sat up looked at the clothes on the end of the bed. She rose up on her knees and embraced Alex. "I told you this wasn't necessary. We don't have to go anywhere. I'm happy anywhere, as long as you're there with me. Just being with you is more than I ever expected."

He held her, reveling in the warmth of her closeness. "Humor me, sweetheart. Go with me, please." He kissed her tenderly on the soft skin just above her breastbone.

"I can't tell you *no* about anything. Did you know that?"

"I'm counting on it, baby girl. You don't know how much I'm counting on it."

Later that night, he made her dreams come true. "I can't believe you bought me all of these beautiful things." Scarlet lay her head on Alex's shoulder, holding on to his arm.

"I enjoy buying you things, love." Pulling into Zilker Park, Alex could see the horse drawn carriage awaiting their arrival.

"Look at the horses, Alex. Could we walk over and look at them?"

"I think that could be arranged." He lifted her out of the Hummer and hand in hand they strolled over to the white carriage.

"Good evening, Mr. Stewart." The driver greeted Alex and handed him the huge bouquet.

When Alex turned to give Scarlet the roses, he found her looking at him in amazement. "These are for me?" She couldn't believe it. There were dozens and dozens of perfect yellow roses.

"And their beauty pales next to yours." Alex had arranged for a large white basket to be mounted across the front of the carriage, just big enough to hold the flowers. Arranging them in the basket for Scarlet, he then, turned and held out his hand to help her up and into the seat.

"I can't believe you did this. I feel like Cinderella." Joyous laughter bubbled out from Scarlet. "I've never done anything like this in my entire life."

"I hoped you would enjoy it, sweetheart. And the night is young. I have several other surprises in store for you." He gathered her close and they settled back to enjoy the view of beautiful Lady Bird Lake and the scenes of downtown Austin, except Alex only had eyes for Scarlet. He was entranced, watching her delight in a simple ride through the park.

"I wish tonight would never end," Scarlet whispered, picking up Alex's hand and kissing the palm.

"It doesn't have to. Tonight *can* go on forever. Stay with me, Scarlet." He hadn't planned on saying this, but he couldn't seem to help himself.

"I wish I could. You don't know how badly I wish I could." As she said this, she couldn't meet his eyes.

"You can. It's simple. Just don't go. I'll take care of you, always." With gentle care he slipped the bracelet onto her wrist. With a gasp, she looked down to see a white gold bangle, completely covered in diamonds.

"Oh, my Lord," Scarlet breathed. "I have never seen anything so fabulous in my entire life."

"Read the engraving," Alex encouraged. He held her hand and pulled the bracelet off so she could read the words. *'Alex loves Scarlet, Today, Tomorrow and Forever'*.

Her first impulse was to show him how much she loved him. And that impulse she couldn't resist. "I love you. I love you. I love you." The driver glanced back and smiled at the sight of the small woman launching herself at the big man.

She rested her cheek against his forehead. "Alex, this is too much, baby." Scarlet cradled the hand that wore the bracelet up to her heart. "You shouldn't have done this. You shouldn't have gotten it engraved. It'll be such a waste."

"Nothing that I could ever give you would be a waste. Don't say that." He knew she meant that she didn't have long to live.

She pulled herself from his lap and kissed the cool silver colored bracelet tenderly. "I didn't mean that, I'm sorry. I love it. It's by far the most beautiful thing that I have ever owned."

The driver turned and gestured to Alex that they had reached the docking port for the supper cruise vessel. "Come on, doll. Time for phase two." He helped her out and picked up the huge basket of yellow roses.

Surprisingly, the captain of the ship handed the keys over to Alex with a smile.

"Thanks. Come aboard, baby."

It was unlike anything she had ever expected. Alex took them out onto the lake and she sat with him under the stars watching the lights of the city go by. Heading for a secluded cove, downstream on the scenic Colorado, he pulled in and cut the engine.

"Now for the good stuff." In the luxurious cabin, he opened and unpacked two large picnic baskets. They were full of delicacies that made their mouths water—crab cakes, stuffed mushrooms, sliced avocados, roasted asparagus and strawberries with chocolate fondue sauce.

"Heavenly." Scarlet licked her lips at the sight of the delicious food.

"Come on, let's eat so we can see the water and the

skyline." She followed his lead and they dined like royalty.

"Alex, can we pretend? Just for tonight." Scarlet asked with a hopeful expression on her face.

"Pretend? I don't understand." Alex wanted to do anything for her that he could, no matter how painful.

"Let's pretend that we, that I, have a future. Just for a few hours, let's dream about what our life would be like." Alex swallowed the pain. Maybe if he went along with this she would see that they did indeed have a future.

"Okay, what do we plan first?" Alex watched her beautiful face, alight with visions of impossible things.

"Our honeymoon." He wondered why she was skipping the wedding, but that was okay, he already had that part handled.

"All right." He gave her a private, wicked grin. "Let's talk about the honeymoon. I have a pretty good idea of what we'll do, but where do you want to go?"

"Somewhere in the RV." She smiled, remembering what wonderful things he had done to her body in that RV.

Getting into the spirit of things, he thought of her bucket list. "I'll take you to Graceland for our honeymoon. Would you like that?"

"Oh, yes. That would be perfect." Standing up, she leaned over and kissed him full on the lips. "When we come home, will we live with Ethan and Annalise?" She tried not to let her personal desires show.

"No way, baby. I'm going to build us our own home on a piece of land that sits right on the banks of the Sabinal River." Alex dipped a strawberry into chocolate and inserted it between her lips. "Soon, I'll drive you out to see it."

"I'd love that. Do you think that I could have an herb garden and a room just for my sewing?" The way they were talking, they had left pretend behind and had moved straight into full reality mode.

"An herb garden, a rose garden and big beds of daylilies," Alex promised her. "And inside we will have home offices for our joint consulting firm, a game room for me, a sewing room for you, a full gourmet kitchen and the biggest most sensual master bed and bath that could possibly be conceived." Scarlet closed her eyes, visualizing their dream house.

"And children?" Scarlet asked. "Would you let me have your baby?"

"God, yes." Alex was as caught up in the fantasy as she was. "Six of them.' At that Scarlet laughed. "Six?"

"Well, two or three, to start with." He placed a hand on her cheek, imagining what a little girl with her sapphire blue eyes and dark curls would look like. "What would we call our little boy?"

"Phillip Alexander, of course," she said with a smile.

"I like that, what about our little girl?"

"Isabella, I think."

"That was my grandmother's name." Alex marveled.

"Well, then, that's settled. Isabella. It's meant to be." She didn't realize what she had said, but Alex did.

"You're right, sweetheart. It's meant to be, all of it. You were sent to me, you were born to be a part of my life. *We* were meant to be, Scarlet." At his solemn words, the skies above them lit up in a myriad of lights and colors.

"Oh, Alex, look! Fireworks!" She walked over to him and climbed onto his lap. "Aren't they beautiful? How lucky we are to be here just at the right time."

"Yeah, lucky." He started to tell her that the fireworks were part of his gift to her, but maybe letting her think that it was providence would work in his favor.

"See how everything is coming together? This night is magical, love."

And it was.

Even more so, when he took her home. To bed.

* * * *

Two days before the wedding…

The next morning, Scarlet woke up first. Her thoughts immediately flew back to the wonderful night that Alex had given her. Had it really happened? The bracelet on her wrist was a testament to the accuracy of her memories. He had brought her home and taken her to his bed. There had been no doubt in her mind when he had finished that his desire for her knew no bounds. This morning, she intended to give him quid pro quo.

He was laying on his back, his magnificent chest bare, the sheet slipping down to just below his waist. There was a mountain on the horizon, however. He had a morning erection that looked like Mt. Everest. She wondered how he would like waking up like Sleeping Beauty—with a kiss. But the kiss that she had in mind wasn't one that would land on his lips.

Carefully, so as not to awaken him, she eased the sheet back. Scarlet bit her lip to keep from moaning out loud at the sight. He was incredible. So proud. So rigid. So swollen. So beautiful. Nothing could have kept her away. She bent over him and gently taking him in her hand, she licked his shaft from bottom to top, following the delectable raphe ridge that ran along the underside. At her caress, Alex lifted his hips, and groaned in his sleep. Pleased with his initial reaction, Scarlet took him in her mouth, luxuriously bathing him with her tongue. She paid special attention to the sensitive glans that made up the bulbous head, tracing her tongue around and around in endless circles. Applying delicate suction, she drew him deep into her mouth, holding the base of his shaft with one hand and caressing his balls with the other.

Alex arched his back off the bed. At first, he thought he was having the most intense erotic wet dream of his life. *Heat—friction—moist creamy haven—Holy Heavens*! Fully awake, he realized that Scarlet was giving him the most incredible wake-up call of his life. Glancing down at her, he met her eyes, which looked at him with so much love and desire that he almost climaxed right then and there. "Sweet, baby girl," he moaned. "What are you doing to me?"

Her answer was to take him deeper and suck him harder. Scarlet couldn't be still, she was trying to alleviate the hunger between her legs by pressing her thighs together. Alex was enchanted. She was as aroused as he was. Despite her concentrated efforts to concentrate on him, he watched her hips began to dip up and down. The motion drew Alex's eye and he couldn't resist. "Oh, you're excited too, aren't you baby?" His hand gravitated to her bottom, slipping his fingers deep within her cleft. When she felt his welcome invasion, her relief manifested itself with a throaty groan. The vocalization of her excitement vibrated all around his super-sensitive cock, and Alex exploded in ecstasy. Scarlet reacted to his incredible pleasure by answering it with a quivering climax of her own. She kissed and loved him with her mouth until she had drained him of every drop of his erotic release.

Alex pulled her up into his arms, cradling her body next to his. "You have got to be the sweetest thing in the whole world. Do you have any idea how much I love you?"

"I know how much I love you. And it's so many things. I'm not talking about the sex. Or just the sex."

Alex chuckled so hard, she was dislodged from his chest.

"Watch the ego, Scarlet," he teased her.

"You know what a great lover you are, you ego isn't dependent on my stroking," she teased back.

"Oh, but you're wrong. I'm very much dependent on your stroking." He rolled her over on top of him and nuzzled her on the neck.

"Listen to me, Alex." She was giggling so hard, trying to get her breath. He eased up so she could finish her thought. "I'm talking about the feelings, the love, the sense of belonging to someone. Even if it was for just a little while. I adore you."

"My sweet baby." He framed her face with his hands, forcing her to look at him. "How in the world do you ever expect me to live even one day without you?"

She didn't answer. What could she say? They only had three more nights, seventy-two hours, before she had to leave. Letting out a long, tortured breath, she nestled against him, wishing for a miracle.

CHAPTER SEVEN

The girls went shopping. Scarlet had to take it easy and sit down every few minutes, but she convinced her sister that it was because she had slept poorly the night before. That hadn't been true. In Alex's arms, she had slept like a baby.

"I want to go to Chico's and Cold Water Creek." Annalise announced. They had pulled into the beautiful Arboretum mall.

"I want to go to Barnes and Nobles and look at our books on the shelves." Cecile was serious. She loved to do that. "What do you want to do, Scarlet?"

There was no doubt in her mind, it was number thirty-three on her bucket list. "Cheesecake Factory," she said with awe and reverence in her voice. The other two girls cracked up. Their day was planned.

* * * *

Alex spent the day at the doctor's office. Doc Gibbs ran him through a battery of tests. They had to be certain that Scarlet's body would accept his kidney. Ethan and Bobby went with him, knowing how very important and serious this was to him. "Don't worry, Alex. Everything's going to be all right. You're going to be a perfect match." Bobby tried to reassure his brother.

"I have to believe that, Bobby." Alex sat in the waiting room, his head in his hands. "Your brother and I have pulled a thousand strings, and I have put Scarlet on my insurance roll at Econ. So I can keep her alive with dialysis and medicine. That is, if she'll let me." Alex's voice cracked. "She just has this hard-headed idea that she doesn't want to be a burden to anyone. I don't know how to make her understand that I can't live without her." Both brothers placed their hands on Alex's back. One sat on one side of him and one on the other. "What I really want for her, though, is a normal life. I want my kidney to be a perfect match, so we can make all of our dreams come true. I want to be married to her for fifty years. I want to show her the world, not just the modest requests on her bucket list. I want to give her everything she deserves. I want children with her." Alex stopped talking. He hated to appear weak in front of his brothers.

They didn't look at it that way, however. Ethan leaned over, close to his brother. "You will, Alex. You will marry her tomorrow, and in a few days, you'll give her a hell of a wedding gift—a future. I know it. I'm praying for it, Bobby and I both are." Bobby voiced his agreement.

"The doctor will see you now." The nurse's simple words brought all three of them to their feet. It might not have been normal, but all three brothers filed into the office, anxious to hear what the verdict was.

If the sight seemed strange to Doc Gibbs, he didn't say so. "Alex," he looked at the largest Stewart brother straight on. "You and Scarlet have a match on only three out of six antigens." At Alex's stricken look, the doctor held up his hand. "No, wait. There's still one more thing to check. We have performed a cross-match test that will tell us the likelihood of Scarlet's body rejecting your kidney. We're hoping for a negative result."

"Negative, how could that be good news?" Alex didn't understand.

"A negative result would mean that the probability of rejection of your kidney would be small. Don't lose hope, in fact, be positive—to not be related, the two of you seem to chemically and physiologically have much in common."

"Well, I could have told you that," Bobby said. "You two were created for each other." Bobby's words gave Alex a tremendous sense of peace.

"You're right, Bobby. Scarlet was created just for me." And he intended to use those words to Scarlet as he presented his case to her. He wasn't naive enough to think that she was going to fall in easily with his plans. She was just too stubborn and too protective of him. Scarlet was going to have to be convinced.

Doc Gibbs wasn't finished, however. "I sent Scarlet's blood off to the premier research laboratory at the University of California. The results should be here this afternoon or in the morning. This will tell us exactly what we're dealing with, how much time we have, and the best way to proceed. Due to malpractice law, I can only call *her* with the results. So stick close to her, just in case she decides not to share with you what I've told her. And I'll call you both as soon as I have the results of the cross-match."

"Thanks, Doc." Alex assured him, forcing himself to remain positive. If he had his way, Scarlet was going to live. Now, if everything fell into place, all he would have to do is convince her to accept his gift of life.

"How much will the transplant cost?" Alex asked taking out his checkbook.

"She doesn't have insurance?" The doctor wasn't really surprised.

"No, I'll be taking care of everything."

"Why don't we wait and see. There's no use paying for something that is just a maybe at this stage."

"No," Alex said. "I believe in the law of attraction. I'm going to act as if this transplant is a done deal. Now, how much?"

"I can't be completely sure, but approximately $375,000, give or take a dollar or two." Alex never hesitated. He wrote the check, tore it out and handed it to the doctor. "We'll divide it up between you and your hospital later, Okay?"

Doc Gibbs knew that this was Alex's way of hanging on to hope. He took the check and placed it in his safe, hoping against hope that he would have reason to cash it.

* * * *

It was time for the cakes. Scarlet had decided to bake the groom's cake first. The cake itself had chocolate syrup and real butter in it. Rich was not the word. The icing was made with heavy cream and chocolate chips, absolutely sinful. "That smells heavenly," Alex murmured as he embraced her from behind. He was holding nothing back. Every waking moment, he conveyed his love and desire for her. And there was no doubt she shared his feelings, loving the attention. In fact, she ate it up.

Turning in his arms, she fitted her body to his. "I made you a small one. You can have it now, if you'd like."

"Thanks, love. That was sweet of you." He fitted his mouth to hers, drinking from her mouth like a man who was starving for a life-giving drink of water.

"Did you actually suppose that I wouldn't think of you? You're always on my mind. I'd do anything for you." She was surprised when he pulled away and reached for a pad and pen. "What are you doing?"

"I'm writing this down," he said playfully. "I'm going to hold you to those words, Scarlet." He actually put pen to paper. "Scarlet Rose Evans says she will do anything for one, Phillip Alexander Stewart. Duly noted. Here sign it."

He held it out to her and she giggled and did as he requested. Then, he put it away for safe keeping.

Scarlet mischievously pushed at him with her bottom, and he reacted as expected. Clasping her bottom with both hands, he pulled her into his heat. "When can you stop? I'm hungrier for you than I am for cake."

"Not for a while, unfortunately. I've got the batter mixed up for the wedding cake, but there's a lot left to do to get it all baked, assembled and decorated." She glanced at the clock on the wall. "I'll be at this till midnight. I'm just grateful that you have these commercial appliances, that alone is going to save me a world of time and effort."

"Let me help," he urged. "I'm as talented as a pastry chef as I am in the bedroom."

"Honey, if you were, they would have you teaching at the French Culinary Institute."

"Am I that good?" Male egos need to be fed.

"Do you have to ask? Aren't my screams of ecstasy testimony enough?" Looking over at him, she saw that ravenous look of lust on his face. "Uh, oh. No time for that. Go, do manly things. You've wasted entirely too much time entertaining me this week." As she said the words, she realized what she had done. His face fell. She had inadvertently reminded him of their meeting, when he had hurt her with his thoughtless words.

"Impossible."

"I didn't mean it, Alex. Stay with me, please." She didn't have to ask again. He followed her directions, and together, they created a masterpiece for his brother and her sister. A masterpiece of love.

After midnight, he carried her to his big claw foot tub. She was exhausted. "Sit here, sweetheart. I'll run us a bath." The tub was huge, a seventy-two inch Randolph Morris. Pure luxury.

"Can we take this tub with us to our house?" Alex looked at her in wonder. Did she know what she was saying?

"I'll buy you one just like it, sweetheart," he assured her. "And I'll give you a bath in it every night." He added bath salts, undressed himself and her, and eased her down into the warm, soft water

He sat at the back of the tub, with her between his legs. "This feels so good, Alex." He took a soft wash cloth and a bar of clean scented soap and began to wash her. It wasn't meant to be sexual, he was simply taking care of her. Gradually, the heat began to build. Alex made no move to initiate anything, but Scarlet did. As he caressed her body with the wash cloth, she ran her hands up and down his strong legs, tracing the muscles, loving how they enfolded her so securely. When she was with Alex like this, it seemed to both of them as if death itself could have no power over their happiness. "Alex, I want you."

He was ready for her. He was always ready. "Hold on, baby." He picked her up, carefully, pulled his legs together and eased her down on top of his shaft. "Guide me in, sweetheart." She leaned her head back on his shoulder and eased her body down onto his.

"Ecstasy," she moaned. Alex did all the work. He pulled her back up against him and with a flexing of his hip muscles, he soon had them delirious with pleasure. Afterwards, he helped her from the tub, patted her dry and carried her to bed. "I love you," Scarlet whispered as he tucked her against him and covered her with the sheet and quilt.

"I love you, too, baby. I love you, too."

* * * *

One day before the wedding…
Dress rehearsal day…
Alex and Scarlet's wedding day…

Alex was as nervous as a cat. Not about marrying Scarlet. He was nervous about how she would react when she discovered that he had manipulated the events of the day to serve his plan.

The first order of the day was to get her to sign the wedding license. Actually, it was a piece of cake. She didn't even question him, but followed his directions to a T. "Sign here, baby. This is the marriage license. You and I are the official witnesses." None of that was a lie, one just didn't have anything to do with the other.

Next, he had to give her the dress that she would marry him in. It was a tea length champagne sheath made of silk and lace with a short bolero jacket made entirely of lace with tiny pearls scattered throughout. It was the most beautiful dress he had ever seen. He found her outside by the pool, going over her list of last minute to-do's. "Hey doll, do you need any help?"

"No, I'm going over the seating chart for the rehearsal dinner tonight, we've had a few cancellations and a few additions. I have to see who I can slip in where. Plus, this is my list of bride's maid chores to do today and tomorrow, and I have to prioritize them." Alex wanted to tell her that a bride shouldn't have to work so hard on her wedding day, but that would have spoiled his sneak attack. But if he was going to get her in the dress, he was going to have to tell her about it.

"I laid a dress out on our bed for you to wear tonight." That was his best plan, just come out and say it.

She put her list down and looked at him straight in the face. "I had a perfectly good dress to wear tonight. It's homemade, but it doesn't look so bad." She said this quickly, as if she thought it had to be said, then she got this tender little look and said, "You bought me a dress?"

"I couldn't bear to see you wear a dress that you

made for another man," he admitted without shame. "Besides, this dress is hot and you're going to look hot *in* it." Before she could protest, he picked her up and marched into the main house with her.

On their way, he expected her to protest, instead she took the opportunity to kiss his neck. "If you didn't have to be in front of so many people today and tomorrow, I would mark you—right here." She teased him by biting him playfully.

"Mark me, baby. I don't care." But, she did. She kissed him gently instead.

When he had her in their room, he lowered her to her feet. She turned and saw the dress. "Oh, Alex." Scarlet had no idea that she walked around with his heart strings wrapped firmly around her pretty little fingers. But it was true. And when she dropped to her knees to look at the dress more closely, she tugged hard on those strings. "What a gorgeous dress! It's beautiful enough to be somebody's wedding dress!" Yes, those strings brought him to his knees right beside her. "Thank you, Alex." But instead of smiling as he wanted her to, she laid her head down on his bed and cried.

"No, baby. Please don't cry." He didn't know what to do. This wasn't the reaction he had been aiming for. "Come here."

"I'm sorry. You're so good to me, Alex." She wiped her eyes, trying to regain her composure. "It was silly of me. I was just wishing that this was our wedding day." Alex had to bite his lip, he wanted to tell her so bad. But, he was afraid that if he did, she wouldn't go through with it. He just couldn't take the risk, it was too important. Her life and their happiness depended on it.

"You're going to be a vision of beauty in this dress. And here are your shoes and new underwear and a necklace that matches your new bracelet." The tears started up anew and this time she held him close. "Let's put your necklace around your pretty little neck."

"It's too much," she whispered. "Are these real diamonds?" she asked reverently.

"I wouldn't buy you anything else." He had found the perfect set for her. The eternity set. The bracelet, necklace and ring meant more to him than just a beautiful gift for a beautiful woman. He was telling her that their love was forever, for eternity. The three pieces had set him back over one hundred sixty thousand dollars and it had been well worth every cent. "You are more precious to me than all the diamonds in the world."

As he fastened the necklace, he kissed the spot where it touched her skin. When he lifted his head, a tear remained. And it glistened brighter than any diamond ever had.

* * * *

Alex found her cell phone on their bed. She wasn't used to carrying one, or she had left it on purpose—he didn't know. So, when his cell rang and Doc Gibbs's name was on the caller ID, he wasn't surprised, just scared to death. "Hello."

"Alex, I can't get through to Ms. Evans. Could you ask her to call me, immediately?"

"You sound concerned." Alex bowed his head in sheer panic.

"Alex, you know I can't say anything. Just have her call me. Now."

He found her, and finally got her to be still. "Stop, Scarlet." Alex held her by the shoulders. "You have got to go call the doctor. Now."

"Why, Alex?" Scarlet was trying to pretend she didn't understand what he was saying. "I already have my pills." He knew she didn't want to know what the doctor had to say.

They both knew what he was going to say.

They could feel it.

Right now, Alex could see that Scarlet was running on pure adrenaline. "Just let me get through the wedding tomorrow, and after that—"

"We can't wait until after the wedding, you need to call him, now. Please, baby. Call the doctor. For me?"

Scarlet closed her eyes. "Why do you have to make it about you? You know I can't deny you anything." Taking the phone from him, she began to dial.

Alex stood there while she phoned the doctor's office. She turned her back to him and talked in a low voice. He couldn't hear the conversation. He didn't have to. He watched the set of her shoulders, one minute they were squared, the next they stooped forward in defeat. She recovered quickly, but he knew.

Her kidney function had fallen to a critical level.

"Tell me, Scarlet."

"Tell you what?"

"The results of the blood tests."

"Let's not spoil the day with talk of doctors and disease."

It nearly killed him, but Alex didn't press it. He'd wait till his ring was on her finger, then they'd have a serious talk.

* * * *

Annalise and Ethan were radiant. The wedding party and close friends began to arrive. Not all of the decorations were up, but there was enough to make the setting enchanting. Bobby and Cecile were holding hands and making goo-goo eyes at each other. Literally. The little Lutheran preacher was a rotund man with a sliver of silver hair that rimmed his head. He addressed the group, and Scarlet thought he seemed extremely nervous. Weddings she knew. And this little man was acting like it was his first rodeo.

"Let's go over the music first. Both songs. Get it out of the way." Scarlet almost laughed. She had no ego involved, so getting her songs out of the way was no big deal. The piano that Alex had rented for her was a great instrument, and with just a few touches, she found her key. She began with *Unchained Melody*. It was for Annalise and Ethan.

A hush fell over the crowd as Scarlet began to sing. Singing and playing the piano was something that came easy for her. Her voice was strong and she lost herself in the words. She sang of love that had been lost, now found. She sang of hunger and desire and a lover's prayer that God would bring them together once more. The songs were meant to be for the bride and groom, but in truth, she would sing to Alex.

Alex was floored, flabbergasted, awe-struck and amazed. He had not doubted that Scarlet could sing. But, he had no idea that her voice would be absolutely incredible. She could have easily been a star. Her voice was blue velvet, lush and smooth as silk. He had been standing, but he had to sit down. And when she began the next song, Elvis's *Love Me Tender*, he knew without a doubt that she was singing right to him. Looking into his eyes, she asked him to love her tender, love her sweet. She asked Alex to never let her go. He wanted to walk to her, assure her that he would hold on to her for the rest of his life, with both hands. But he forced himself to be still. She told him that he had made her life complete and that she loved him more than words could tell. With tears flowing down her cheeks, she asked him to make all of her dreams come true. There would never be a dearer moment in his memory than when she sang just to him, promising that she would love him forever. He intended to hold her to it. When she had finished, he walked to her.

"Why didn't you tell me you could sing like that?" Alex pulled her to one side and into his arms.

"It's no big deal, I've sung like that for years." She brushed aside his complement.

"You could have easily had a career in music," he persisted.

She looked at him with sad eyes. "I didn't want a career in music. I want…" She couldn't bring herself to finish the sentence. "It's time to line up, Pastor Ron is giving us the evil eye."

"Let him wait. I want to hold you a minute before we begin the ceremony."

She leaned into him, resting against his shoulder. "It's just a rehearsal, no big deal."

"It is a big deal, darlin'. A solemn ceremony. We're going to be standing in front of a man of God and saying words of devotion and commitment. Before we do, I want to tell you how very much I love you." Alex rubbed her temple, easing a lock of hair off of her forehead, then kissed her once softly on the lips.

"I love you, too."

Reaching behind his back, Alex handed her a beautiful white rose. "Carry this for me, sweetheart, and don't forget, Scarlet, we love each other. Now, it's time. Let's take our places."

The music began and Alex, Ethan and Bobby walked from the right side of the rose bed to the front of the arbor. Alex was playing the part of the groom, a role that would be reversed the following day. As the music continued, Cecile stepped out to walk slowly down the aisle. She and Bobby only had eyes for each other. Annalise came next and she blushed like a school girl as Ethan winked at her. After she and Cecile were in their places, the music swelled and Alex looked up to see his angel standing in a golden ray of the evening sun. He had never seen anything or anyone more beautiful. Slowly, she walked toward him. He knew she thought this was just a rehearsal, but he knew her well enough to know that she was imagining this was real. That it was their wedding day.

When she drew close enough, he held out his hand to help her up on the dais.

"Dearly Beloved, we are gathered here tonight to join this man and this woman in holy matrimony." Alex picked up Scarlet's right hand in his and brought it to his lips. The preacher continued.

"A marriage ceremony like this is for one purpose only and that is to make one flesh from two people that love and cherish one another above all things. At this time, Alex and Scarlet wish to take this step. They have chosen one another out of all others in this life and now they stand before us ready to repeat their vows. Alex."

Scarlet's eyes were darting around nervously, Alex knew she had been to enough wedding rehearsals to know this one was not proceeding as normal. Still, she did not bolt and run. Alex held on to her hand, looked into her eyes and began.

"I, Phillip Alexander Stewart, take you, Scarlet Rose Evans, to be my lawful wedded wife. I promise to love, honor and cherish you," he paused almost unable to go on. "Till death do us part. I promise to be true and faithful to you for better or worse, in sickness and in health, for as long as we both shall live." Scarlet's eyes were big and focused on every syllable that was coming from his lips. "All of my worldly goods to thee I endow and with my body I will worship yours. I love you, Scarlet. To marry you is my greatest desire." Alex became aware that Scarlet's hand was shaking in his.

"Scarlet." The pastor indicated that it was her turn.

Scarlet looked over at her sister, who had tears in her eyes. Then, she turned back to look at him—to understand. He knew that all she could see on his face was utter devotion—the most sincere look of love that a man could ever give to a woman.

She only hesitated for a moment, but it was a lifetime for Alex. It felt as if his heart was about to escape from his chest. By now, she must realize that this was more than just a rehearsal for Ethan and Annalise. By now, she had to know.

* * * *

Scarlet's mind and emotions were topsy-turvy. Could this really be happening, or were her heart-felt fantasies making more of this than it actually was? With a soft touch, Alex caressed the hand he held. Scarlet took that as a gentle urging for her to say her part. Holding Alex's gaze, she began to speak. "I, Scarlet Rose Evans, take you, Phillip Alexander Stewart, as my lawfully wedded husband. I promise to love, honor, and cherish you, till death do us part." Her voice cracked just a bit, and Alex's hold on her hand tightened, as if giving her courage to continue. "I promise to be true and faithful to you. For better, for worse, for richer or poorer, in sickness and in health, for as long as we both shall live."

Scarlet paused again, her eyes big question marks, and Alex nodded his head, as if telling her that she was doing great. "All my worldly goods to you I give, and with my body I will worship yours. Alex, I adore you, and marrying you would make all my dreams come true."

Alex noted the futuristic wording of her last sentence.

"Is there a ring?"

"Yes, there is." Alex reached into the pocket of his coat. He brought out a glimmering eternity band and slipped it on her finger. "Scarlet, with this ring, I thee wed. With this ring, I offer you my heart, my life, my trust and my eternal devotion."

"I don't have a ring for you," she whispered.

In answer, he just kissed the ring on her finger.

"You may kiss the bride."

Slowly, Alex drew her to him. It was a tender kiss, a slow meeting of the lips, a cherished moment of complete peace and love. Pulling back, Alex gave her the sweetest smile that she could have ever envisioned.

"By the power vested in me by the great state of Texas, I now pronounce you man and wife." Turning them to face the crowd, he announced. "It is my pleasure to be the first to you introduce you as, Mr. & Mrs. Alex Stewart." A crescendo of music followed and Alex swept Scarlet down the central passageway, past prying eyes and countless questions.

He picked her up and held her close. "Oh, my darling. I love you so." He kissed her then, stealing her breath, as he had already stolen her heart. Boldly. Voraciously. She kissed him back, and then laid her forehead against his chest to get her composure.

"That seemed very real, Alex." She didn't know exactly what to say, but she was holding on to him with both hands, just as tight as she could.

"It was real, baby. Very real."

They stood still, he braced himself for her reaction, not knowing what to expect. There was a moment of silence, and then much to Alex's shock and amazement, Scarlet stood on her tiptoe, wrapped her arms around his neck and began to cry. "I don't understand, but I love you. This is the most incredible moment of my life. Explain, please. What does this mean?"

Picking her up, Alex walked swiftly to the house. He carried her straight to his room, so he could be sure that they would be undisturbed. Sitting on the bed, he held her to his chest. "Scarlet, I know I'm probably treading on thin ice, love. But, there was no way that I was letting you walk out of my life. I had to make you understand that you have a future, with me." He placed something in her hand.

"What is this?" she asked in a tear-streaked voice.

"Look at it, babe." His words were said with enough hope and commitment that it was a tangible presence in the air.

Scarlet dropped her eyes, and for a moment, she didn't seem to comprehend what she was holding. It was a card, a plastic card that was engraved with her name, or her new name—Scarlet Evans Stewart. Scarlet turned it over and over. It was emblazoned with the name of Alex's company and a prominent, national insurance carrier. "An insurance card?"

Scarlet looked up at him in wonder. "I can live?"

Her simple little question almost brought him to his knees. "Yes, baby. You can live. With me. Forever."

* * * *

"I can't believe you got married first!" Annalise teased her sister, playfully.

"I can't either," Scarlet admitted, her voice quivering.

"I just knew that you two would get together, there never was a doubt in my mind."

"I never hoped, I never dreamed," Scarlet's voice shook. She still did not intend to reveal her problems to Annalise. Not until she was sure that everything was going to be all right. But, for the first time, she understood that there was a good possibility she was going to be okay. She had a reason to plan, to hope, to dream. And it was all because of Alex.

He stood watching her, even now. Every time she

looked up, his gaze would be upon her. The rehearsal dinner was in full swing. There was no sneaking away, not even for the newlyweds. Minutes and hours passed in a swirl of activity, but finally the time came when they could be alone. "Come with me, sweetheart. It's time for your wedding night." She placed her hand in his, but they didn't walk toward the B&B. Instead, he led her to the side drive and she was shocked to see a limousine sitting there. "It's only for one night, we have to be back tomorrow, but I wanted you to myself for a few hours."

A uniformed chauffeur opened the door and they climbed inside. As soon as the door was shut, he pulled her to him. "I've been wanting to do this all evening." He placed heated kisses from her chin, down the length of her throat, all the way to the tender cleft between her breasts. "You are absolutely luscious."

"Alex, talk to me, please. Tell me what all of this means." She had to ask, she couldn't wait.

"What are you talking about, love? We're married. As married as two people can get, unless..." and he stopped, as if afraid to put his thought into words. "Unless, you don't want to be married to me."

"I want to be married to you more than anything in the world," she assured him. "But I just need to understand what's going on. Exactly. I mean, do you want me to stay here with you or do you intend for me to go back to my house in Pine Forest and just use the card there. If that's what you intended, know that I am grateful—"

She didn't get to complete her sentence. He stopped the progress of her little speech with his lips. "Sweetheart. I want you here, with me. Don't you understand, yet? I want us to be a normal, happily married couple with a house and a yard and a future."

"Are you sure? My illness is going to be a lifetime

struggle. When I begin dialysis, it's going to be a never-ending, day-in-day-out grind."

"Until you get a transplant."

"The likelihood of me getting a transplant is infinitesimal, you know that," she said softly.

"Not if—"

They were both trying to talk at the same time. Finally Scarlett held up her hand to interrupt him. "Does the insurance cover both dialysis and a transplant?"

Closing his eyes, he told the truth, with a sigh. "I'm not going to lie to you. "No, unfortunately. Just dialysis. Even though I own the company, there was only so much lee-way that I had with the insurance company. Since you have a pre-existing condition, I was blessed and very fortunate to get you covered for both medicine and dialysis. But, that doesn't mean that a transplant won't be the next step." He stopped there with his explanation.

"That's okay. This is enough. I am just so grateful. It's more than I ever hoped for." She scooted next to him, and he cuddled her close. "But the best part is getting to stay with you, being married, getting to wake up by you every morning, and going to sleep by you every night."

"I can't wait to start a life with you." He picked up her hand and looked at the eternity band that he had placed on her finger. "Do you want to know where we're going right now?"

"Yes, but I'll be happy with you, no matter where we go." Although she did peep outside the window of the limo to see which direction they were headed in.

"I've booked the Renaissance Bridal Suite at the Driskill Hotel." At her look of joy, he pulled her over onto his lap.

"I'm costing you so much money." Scarlet touched the jewelry he had given her. "This wonderful jewelry must have cost a fortune and I know that you must have moved Heaven and Earth to get me on your insurance roll."

"When are you going to realize that there is nothing that I wouldn't do for you?" He looked at her tenderly. "As for the insurance card, I've got to warn you that you are registered not only as my wife, but as my partner. You, Mrs. Stewart, are the newest employee of Stewart Environment Incorporated."

"I will work so hard for you, I won't let you down, I promise." She looked at him sincerely.

"There's not a doubt in my mind," he assured her. "I look forward to working with you...and living with you...and sleeping with you...and making love to you." He punctuated each proclamation with a kiss and a tickle to her ribs. She was laughing uncontrollably by the time he was through.

The limousine pulled to a stop and Scarlet realized that they had arrived at the beautiful Driskill hotel in downtown Austin. "I didn't bring any night clothes," whispered Scarlet.

"You won't need any," Alex whispered back with a chuckle. "But, I have you something to wear, anyway. Plus, an outfit to wear home tomorrow."

"You think of everything, Alex." She walked beside him proudly as they made their way to the check in desk.

"I try, sweetheart. I try."

CHAPTER EIGHT

The honeymoon suite was out of this world. "This looks like a room fit for a princess."

"That's right, princess." He led her into the gorgeous room where a beautiful four poster canopy bed was showcased on gleaming hardwood floors. He watched amused as she darted around the room, oohing and ahhing over every detail. "Look at the balcony! Look at the—my God! Look at the bathroom!" It was obvious this was a totally new experience.

"Since we ate at the rehearsal dinner, I thought it would be nice if we had our dessert here." At the word dessert, she turned her attention to the dome covered silver trays.

"Chocolate?"

"Of course. Chocolate cheesecake to be exact." He watched her eyes light up. "Do you want some?" Starting toward the table, she surprised him when she suddenly changed course.

"I'd rather have you for dessert."

Her words caused his cock to spring to attention with a life of its own. His angel had a look of absolute bedevilment in her eyes.

"Are you sure you feel like it?" It was only his love talking, his body was already on the same page as her erotic suggestion.

"Knowing that I have a gorgeous new husband, a wonderful new life and a good shot at a future has suddenly given me a burst of energy that I really don't know what to do with…other than this." She sexily sauntered up to him and began unbuttoning his white silk shirt. "Just look at the strong muscular planes of this chest—you are eye-candy, Alex. Pure eye-candy." He chuckled, but he let her play. "I have never seen a man so superbly built, a perfect male specimen in prime condition." She smoothed the palms of her hands down his body. He felt her hands still. "You're trembling. Baby, are you all right, are you cold?" She asked him, her concern evident on her face.

"No," he cupped her face. "I'm not cold. I'm awed and electrified. Do you know why?" She waited for his answer. "I get to make love to my beloved *wife* for the first time tonight."

His words seemed to enflame her. She continued to disrobe him, gently pushing him steadily backward at the same time, toward the huge bed. He let her have her way with him. Being pushed around was not Alex's forte, but with her he was as malleable as sponge cake. "Lay down my handsome husband. I would like to divest you of your pants." It was a hot moment, and she was just so damn cute.

"Divest me of my underwear, too, baby. It's getting a little tight." His wish was her command. She slowly peeled down his black dress pants and let her breath hiss out as she uncovered the silk briefs that appeared to be painted on his swollen and engorged member.

"I love this part of you so much." She took the elastic waistband of his undershorts in both hands and pulled. Sinking to her knees in front of him, she bent over and kissed the blatantly aroused flesh.

"That part of me is quite fond of you, also," he managed to croak.

Scarlet had never been so happy, she was full of hope and joy and peace and it all brimmed over into an avalanche of passion—all directed at the man who loved her enough to give her a lifetime of tomorrows. Standing up, she began to undress slowly. Never before had she had a seductive bone in her body, but now it seemed the floodgates had opened and emotions that had been on permanent ice had melted and were overflowing from every pore of her body. Alex's eyes were locked on her as she began pulling off the bolero jacket, letting it fall to the floor. Later, she would pick it up and carefully fold it, but right now there were more important things to be done. The sheath slid easily up and over her head and when Alex saw her body clad in the shear, lacy, pale-pink bra and the matching lacy panties she watched him swallow hard. "You are so beautiful, Scarlet."

She left the bra and panties on, unable to keep her hands off him any longer. With a slight nip, she captured his lower lip between her teeth and sucked at it playfully, giving him no time to reciprocate. Sliding her lips down his throat, she adorned his shoulders with kisses and kitten-like laps of her tongue. When she reached his well-defined pecs, she paused to pay special attention to his small flat nipples, eliciting a harsh intake of breath. A happy trail of soft, golden hair started at his midriff and led down to the proud evidence of his desire. Scarlet followed that line, caressing him with her mouth and tongue. A whimper of need escaped her lips as she angled his penis to accept her tribute.

* * * *

Alex couldn't take it. He was about to explode. Never had he been more excited than he was now. "Scarlet, baby." He laid back and literally writhed in ecstasy. "Sweetheart, it's my turn." Somehow, he managed to lift himself up and switch their positions. What she'd been doing to him had been the sweetest torture, but he didn't want to be put temporarily out of commission so soon on his wedding night. He wanted this night to be perfect. For her.

"But I was having such a good time," she pouted sweetly.

"So was I, love, too good. But lay back and let me love you, I promise you that in a few moments, you'll be happy you did." Slowly and tenderly, he removed her bra and panties, allowing himself only one sweet kiss to each nipple, before beginning his trek southward. Later tonight, he promised himself he would feed at her breasts for as long as he wanted to, but right now, the throttle was set too high to pull back. Spreading her legs wide, he took a moment to look at her. She was as smooth as silk and as pink as a delicate orchid. Already wet with passion's nectar, he ran an appreciative finger from the top of her sensitive cleft to the bottom.

"Alex, I ache for you, baby. I feel so empty and needy."

"Patience, doll." Easier said than done, he was holding on by the smallest of measures. But the task before him was a pure delight. Taking her hips in his hands, he pulled her forward and began to pay homage to her feminine treasure. He kissed her all around the outer lips of her labia. "So sweet," he murmured. He started out slow, intending to savor and satisfy, but his hunger and excitement took over and he began to consume her with a near mindless voracity.

Scarlet held on to the quilt, as if for dear life. Alex imagined and hoped that spirals of white-hot pleasure were rocketing through her body. She lifted her hips rhythmically, seeking to meet the piercing thrusts of his tongue as he delved into her quivering channel. "Alex!" she shouted as her climax exploded with a tidal wave of sensation. For the first time, Alex was where he could witness the evidence of Scarlet's bliss. He had heard that some females were able to ejaculate, but none of the women he'd ever been with had reached that plateau of excitement. That Scarlet had, sent his heart into a tailspin. He eagerly lapped up the liquid of passion that spilled forth from her pulsating core. "That's it, my baby. Come for me." He stayed with her until she lay, replete. By then, his cock was so hard he could have used it as a pile-driver.

Alex joined her on the bed and held her for a minute until her trembling subsided. "Thank you, my love," she turned to him and pressed every inch of her body as tight into his as she could. "I want to feel you all the way up and down. You make me feel so welcome, so at home, I've never felt like this before. I have a place to be. It's so amazing to know that I have someone who wants to be with me. If I'm not making sense, forgive me. I'm just overflowing with love and emotion. Make love to me, Alex. I want you inside me. Please?"

Alex was incoherent with need. He lay on his back and urged her to straddle him. "Ride me, baby." With shaking hands he held her up high enough so he could slip inside of her. Every time he entered Scarlet he was struck anew by the total perfection of the act of loving her. She was tight, hot, and made just for him. Her vastly talented interior muscles massaged his shaft in ways that boggled his mind. "Lord, Scarlet, what you do to me!"

Gripping her hips, one in each hand, he kneaded their firmness, pushing and pulling her backwards and forwards, creating an intoxicating friction. Watching her breasts bounce was too big of a temptation to resist. Sitting up, he clasped her right breast in his hand and brought it to his lips. Opening his mouth wide, he fitted it over the entire nipple and areola, drawing them in deeply, laving and sucking to his heart's content—tender ministrations designed to send rivulets of pleasure straight to her womb. Scarlet cradled his head to her, kissing him repeatedly on the top of his head.

"Lay me down, Alex. I need to feel you on me." Picking her up, he did as she asked. Reconnecting them, he lay down on top of her, careful to support his weight so as not to crush her. Still, he let his body graze hers, letting her feel his dominant, solid presence as close as she wanted. He thrust into her, ever mindful of her fragile state and his powerful build. But, she wanted no more of careful or holding back. Looking him straight in the eye she lifted her legs and wrapped them around his waist and made his day. "Faster, baby. Harder, love. Make this a wedding night to remember." Burying his head in her neck, he pumped into her, lifting them both beyond the distant stars.

Later, there was chocolate cheesecake. They fed each other on the balcony, watching the moon as it hovered low in the clear Texas sky. Even later, the huge, rainfall shower did not go to waste, and Scarlet grew to appreciate Alex's football shoulders and wrestler's legs. He held her up easily under the warm spray, her legs wrapped around his waist, as he made love to her against the marble wall.

And when they lay beneath the covers, Alex slipped down in the bed until his face was even with her soft, ripe swells. As he had promised himself, he breast-fed from her creamy flesh until they were aching to make love again. Finally, they slept, absolutely and utterly contented.

"Wake up, precious girl. It's time to go home." Scarlet was snuggled in his arms, her back to his front. Upon hearing him whisper in her ear, she stretched in his arms and cuddled close.

"I wish we could stay longer. This has been so wonderful, Alex."

"I promise you that we'll come back." He ran his finger down her nose, and then clasped her to him, running his hands up and down her body. "There are so many things that I want us to do together. We're going to have a wonderful life, baby."

* * * *

"Did you have a good time?" Annalise slyly glanced at her sister.

"Do you have to ask?" Scarlet came back just as playfully.

"These Stewart men are incredible lovers." Cecile agreed, as she joined the pair in the master bedroom. Scarlet blushed in spite of herself, she wasn't as used to sex talk as the other two.

There was still plenty to do and Scarlet rushed around playing the role of the maid of honor, making sure that everything was taken care of. The flowers arrived and the caterer started setting up the wet bar. The band came and did a preliminary set up of their sound equipment and tested it out. Alex was just as busy as Scarlet, but periodically he would catch her and pull her aside for a private moment.

"How are you feeling? Don't push yourself. If you need to rest, just tell someone else what to do." It felt so good to have someone be concerned about her. She was tired, but she didn't let on to Alex. He had enough to worry about, without her adding to his burden.

"I feel like a new bride." She pulled his head down for a kiss. "I'm fine. Right now, I'm heading back into the house to find Annalise's bridal book to put out for the guests to sign. She and Cecile have left to go to the hair salon."

"You didn't want to go and get yours done?" Like a man, Alex had to ask the wrong question.

Scarlet looked stricken. "No. Should I have? I was just going to throw some hot curlers in it? Do you think that will be all right?"

He grabbed her hands and held her still. "You are beautiful, you don't need to do a thing. I wasn't trying to imply that you needed to get your hair done." He laughed, and she realized they were having a typical *couple* conversation. "Go, gorgeous. Do what you need to do and know that you are the most beautiful woman here." He leaned into whisper to her. "Including the bride." Scarlet kissed him again, before heading to the main house.

Alex took the opportunity to call Doc Gibbs and make sure they were on for the first dialysis consultation the following morning. After the wedding, he and Scarlet had some serious things to discuss.

* * * *

Scarlet looked first in Annalise's bedroom, but the book wasn't there. Standing still a moment, she considered where else she might look. Taking one step toward the hall, she walked straight into somebody. It was a man. At first, she assumed it was Alex, and almost put her arms around him. But, then her body, so used to Alex's touch, instinctively knew that this individual was too soft and not broad enough. Backing up a step, she looked up to apologize. Recognition was her first reaction, then a wave of uncomfortable trepidation assailed her. "Rick?"

"That's right, church mouse." Rick didn't give her a chance to get away. He grabbed her roughly by the shoulder and spun her around, pinning her arm painfully behind her back.

Scarlet gasped from the pain. "Why? What do you want?"

"*Want* isn't the right word, Crip. I could never *want* a woman like you. No man in his right mind would ever *want* a woman like you. Alex Stewart doesn't *really* want you." Scarlet struggled and Rick increased the pressure. "You had better be still, or I'll break this arm—snap it like a twig. Does that hurt?"

"Yes, it hurts. But, you're wrong! Alex loves me."

Scarlet stated emphatically. At her declaration, LeBeau pulled the trapped arm up sharply, causing Scarlet to nearly pass out from the pain.

"I told you, one more word like that and I'll do more than dislocate your shoulder. All of this is a joke, church mouse. We're in cahoots, Alex and me. " Rick said with a sneer. "Just like when you thought you would be attending the prom. You're not really married. Who would want to marry you? The truth will eventually come out and everybody will laugh and laugh at you. The church mouse getting a man? Alex is going to enjoy the look on your face when he tells you that this was all a great big hoax. Your hot-shot boyfriend is really in love with your sister and I have proof. He doesn't really love you, you're a stand-in. Listen to this, church mouse."

Still holding on to her, Rick took a small recorder out of his pocket and pressed play. Alex's voice came over it, unmistakable. "I don't love Scarlet. I don't want to marry her. I love Annalise."

Scarlet shut her eyes as the pain assailed her. God, what was she going to do? Was it all a lie? As one who is dying, Scarlet's last few days flashed before her eyes. Alex loved her, didn't he? "Alex loves me." Scarlet stated, but not with as much certainty as before. Suddenly, Rick jerked her hair back sharply, bringing her to her knees. Scarlet bowed her head, not knowing what the next moment would bring. "What do you want from me, Rick?" she asked with resignation in her voice. Lord, she hoped he didn't have a gun. Scarlet never even considered calling for help, there was no way she would knowingly lead anyone else into danger. She would just ride this out, find out what he wanted, and then, hopefully, he would let her go.

"I want what you had. Did you know that your daddy was really mine? Oh, he came off like a big

Christian man, but he had two women and two families. Only, I was hidden. I was cast aside. You, you ugly, bitch, you're my half-sister. And I hate your guts. I want you to be miserable. If you're miserable, I can be happy. Now, I want you to admit that you've gone too far. You're assuming too much. Admit that you don't deserve to be happy." A rivulet of fear traveled down Scarlet's spine as Rick Lebeau's hands slid from her hair to her neck. "Shall I squeeze the breath from your body? How does this feel? Can you breathe?"

At first it was a caress, which turned Scarlet's stomach, but then his fingers tightened around her neck and for the first time, Scarlet feared for her life. How ironic. If what he said was true, her own brother was going to kill her. Somehow, she wasn't shocked. She always knew that life with her father was not what it should be. He always came off as so self-righteous. Perhaps, he had protested *too* much. Now, it looked like it might be all over. She had been prepping her mind for months, readying herself to accept her mortality. What a shame that just as it seemed she would have a real chance at life, another cruel twist of fate seemed destined to take it away. "Why do you care so much? What my father did to you wasn't my fault. I never knew anything about it!"

Suddenly it all made some horrible form of sense. Jeff Ramsey and his hatred for Annalise, Rick LeBeau and his hatred of her. Her father's harsh attitude toward her clubfoot and her kidney disease. It was all connected. His grip on her neck was suddenly a vise and Scarlet knew that she needed to do something if she wanted to live.

"I despise weak people like you, church mouse. The world would be better off without you. I can't resist, I have to hit you. It's going to feel so good. I hate you for taking my daddy away from me, I hate you for having the family that I never had." Rick's voice iced over and he let go of her neck long enough to land a blow against her temple.

Scarlet gulped with pain and then she spoke in a small, defeated voice. "My childhood wasn't anything to write home about. You, of all people ought to know that." With another crushing blow, he hit her again. Desperate, she asked. "If I say what you want me to say, will you let me go?"

"I can't promise anything, but let's try it, sis." Rick's mind was obviously affected. He kept one hand around her throat and the other kept an unforgiving pressure on her arm and elbow. "Say, I am nobody."

"I am nobody."

"Say, No man will ever want me."

"No man will ever want me."

* * * *

Alex had been watching the house and knew that Scarlet had had ample time to find what she needed and return to the yard. An uneasy feeling was niggling at his mind. Unable to shake it, he went to see about her.

Entering the house, he heard voices. Scarlet's he recognized, and the other sounded oddly familiar. Following the sound, he couldn't believe his ears. What the hell? When he rounded the corner and saw that monster LeBeau with his cruel grip on Scarlet, he almost vaporized with fury. And when he heard what that shit was making her say, he lunged.

"You let her go, you piece of trash!" Seeing Alex, the former Longhorn linebacker, rushing him, LeBeau slung Scarlet to one side like so much cotton batting. "What do you mean treating her like that? What did she ever do to you?" Alex didn't give him time or air to answer, he picked him up and flung him out in the hall, and when he landed in a heap, Alex followed him and repeated the process. As soon as he got him outside the B&B, Alex called Bobby over to hold his ex-employee, while he returned to find his baby. God, if that idiot had hurt her, he would kill him with his bare hands.

"Scarlet, baby!" Alex called out, rushing to where he had last seen her. She sat where LeBeau had left her, an almost blank look on her face. "Are you all right?" Alex knelt at her side, his hands lifting her hair to see the damage that the rough hands had done to her soft skin. There were black and blue fingerprints on her neck, and an angry welt was beginning to show itself on her right temple. "I'm so sorry, sweetheart. I'm so sorry. Let me carry you to bed, you need to lie down. I'll call the doctor."

"No. No. That won't be necessary. I'm all right. Just a little bruised that's all." He pulled her to him, but something was wrong. Scarlet held herself back just a little, a tiny stiffness that sent a chill deep into Alex's soul.

"Scarlet, what's wrong?" Alex asked with fear in his heart.

"I'm fine," she answered softly. Scarlet looked at Alex, with a confused, disoriented expression on her face, as if she kept waiting for him to explain what had happened. "He didn't really hurt me. He told me that he was my half-brother. Do you think he's telling the truth?" Scarlet's voice was vague and disconnected. She was scaring Alex to death. "I think he was just trying to scare me, that's all."

"Your brother? You've got to be kidding me! Tell me everything. What did he say to you?" Alex helped her up, still trying to examine her body. He found the marks on her arm and noticed that she kept it protectively against her, as if it brought her pain. Something was wrong. It was more than just her physical injuries. Scarlet should be clinging to him, letting him comfort her. Instead, it was if she were somewhere else. She had withdrawn from him.

"I don't know," she shrugged. "He just wanted me to admit that I was nobody important and that I had no right to be happy." Her voice sounded so distant, as if her mind was otherwise occupied. Scarlet was answering the questions automatically, without feeling or emotion.

"Talk to me, Scarlet. What's wrong? I can tell something has happened besides the obvious." Alex was desperate. He couldn't fix it if he didn't know what was broke.

Alex was chilled when Scarlet turned to him and smiled a little far-away smile. "Everything will be all right. Let's go down and tend to the wedding preparations. We'll sort all of this out later."

Bobby had called 911 and LeBeau had been arrested for trespassing and for assault and battery. Scarlet had been cooperative, but Alex could tell that something had changed. She was saying all the right things, but her heart wasn't reaching her voice. He hovered near her, touching her at every opportunity. She never flinched from his touch, but she offered none of her own. The timing was piss-poor. There was no place and no opportunity to talk to her, he would just have to wait until after the wedding and reception to get her alone and get to the bottom of this mess.

* * * *

Scarlet didn't know what to think. Everything had been so wonderful, so perfect. And now? Now she wasn't so sure. She needed to be alone and work it all out in her mind. Alex wasn't acting any different, he was as loving and attentive as ever. But, if this were all a joke, if everything he had said and done had been a farce, Scarlet thought she just might die. Funny. If this were a joke, then so was the insurance card. Something in her rebelled, there was no way that Alex could be that cruel.

But Rick LeBeau was a different story. He had always hated her, and now she knew why. In their scant dealings, he had always been the aggressor, and she had never knowingly antagonized him about anything. It was intimidating to realize that you irritated someone else just by being alive.

Scarlet stood at her spot at the garden gate, welcoming each guest, making sure everyone knew where the restrooms were and where to put their wraps. No one seemed to notice the bruising, she had hid it well with make-up.

Alex was advising the parking attendants and greeting business associates, but he checked on her every few minutes. Everything that Rick had said to her and the tape he had made her listen to was playing and replaying in her head. Alex wasn't in love with Annalise, he was in love with her...wasn't he?

Scarlet mechanically took care of business. Questions and variables were hurdling through her mind like ricocheting bullets. On her way to take her place with the rest of the wedding party, her cell phone beeped in her bejeweled evening bag. Who could possibly be calling? There wasn't anyone else that would call her. "Hello?"

"Is this Scarlet Evans?"

"Yes."

"You probably don't remember me, but this is Sandy Moffett at the County Clerk's office. I just called to let you know there was a problem with that marriage license that was filed for yours and, uh, Alex's nuptials."

"A problem?"

"Yes, I don't have all the information, but I wanted to call and let you know that you aren't married." Was that a muffled laugh that she heard? "You will need to reapply for a new license. I hope this isn't a tremendous inconvenience."

"Have you contacted Alex?" Scarlet's voice was weak and she had to force herself to speak up loud enough for the woman to hear her.

"I've tried, but so far, I haven't been able to get through. Could you let him know?"

"I'm sorry, but that won't be possible. Could you keep trying his cell?"

Scarlet knew who Sandy Moffett was. She was the woman who had made no secret in her attraction to Alex. Oh, God! Scarlet felt like she was going to throw up. Her legs were weak and she was trembling all over. God, it was true! There was no wedding. Alex didn't love her and she had been the brunt of the most elaborate punk of the century. How they must be laughing! What would Annalise say? Tears welling up in her eyes, Scarlet sought a quiet place to shelter her nervous breakdown. Heading into the pool house, she thrust the door open and sank to her knees. How could she face Alex, now?

Flashes of memory kept invading her thoughts—the touch of Alex's hands and lips upon her body, the rapture they had shared. How could he have faked that? He had been attracted to her or there was no way he could have made love to her like he did. Something wasn't right. Trying to pull herself together, she tried to separate what she knew from what she thought she knew. Reliving every moment that she had spent with Alex, she tried to remember even one time when there was a hint that he did not love her. There was none. Either he was the greatest actor since Clark Gable or he was sincere. And that meant that Rick LeBeau was responsible for the whole thing.

There was one character trait that Scarlet had always prided herself on, and that was the ability to view the facts and then face them for what they were. After analyzing the horrible events from every angle, Scarlet made a decision.

She had no reason to doubt Alex.

He said he loved her, and he had shown her that he did in every possible way.

So, Scarlet decided to believe him.

Unwilling to wait another moment, Scarlet went to find her husband. As she walked out of the pool house, a sight greeted her that took her right back to square one. Standing before her was Alex, and in his arms was Sandy Moffett. Unable to bear the sight of him in the arms of another woman, she stole quietly away.

* * * *

"Sandy, I told you that this wedding was private." Once again, Alex was trying to extricate himself from the blonde's clutches.

"I knew you didn't mean it. You want me here." She ran her fingers through his hair, he pulled her hands down. "Tell me the truth Alex, aren't you even tempted to kiss me?"

"No, I'm not. I am a happily married man." Alex was emphatic in his rejection of her.

"Well, that's not exactly true." Sandy said with a twinkle in her eye. "There was a problem with the license. It was rejected." Sandy's words were said so flat and commonplace that at first Alex didn't digest them.

"What did you say?"

"You aren't married to that woman, Alex. Your special license was rejected. Don't ask me the details,

I'm just a lowly clerk." If Alex hadn't been in public, he might have been tempted to throttle the bitch standing before him. If the special license had been rejected, he knew it had been her doing.

"Well then, I'll just have to see that it gets fixed. Won't I?" He stepped back from the poisonous woman, her very presence turning his stomach. "Can you see yourself off of my property or would you like my help?" He stared at her cold and hard. Sandy should be able to tell by the steely determination in his eyes that Alex was deadly serious about her leaving. So, she left.

Alex scanned the crowd, looking for Scarlet, but she was nowhere to be seen. He wanted her to know nothing of what had just transpired. He would move Heaven and Earth to fix this. Scarlet had been through enough today. All he wanted to do was get this ceremony behind him, go to the police station and take care of the LeBeau crap and come back so he could be alone with his wife.

The parking was done and the guests were taking their places. Soon, it would be time for him to join his brothers and the pastor to wait for their cue to begin the wedding ceremony. Dressed in an Armani tux, Alex supposed he looked pretty good. Surveying the crowd, he couldn't miss the stares of the women as they watched him hungrily. But he didn't give a damn. The only pair of eyes he wanted watching him were Scarlet's.

Taking a deep breath, he looked around to search for her. Before, he could take another step, a small pair of hands slipped around his waist. Relief washed over him like a warm spring rain. "Would you hold me, please?" Her simple request was the sweetest words he had ever heard.

Turning to her, he pulled her close and pressed butterfly kisses all over her face. "Gladly." His heart was hammering as if he had run a marathon. Now this was more like it.

Scarlet held him tightly. She didn't understand, and she didn't know what was going to happen. What she needed was time to think, alone, away from Lost Maples and away from Alex. So, what he didn't know was that this was good-bye, at least for a little while. "I just wanted to tell you thank you for everything you have done for me." She let him hold her tight, and she allowed herself to sink into his hard warmth one more time.

"This will soon be over, baby. I have to go take care of business at the police station, but just as soon as I can, I'll come home to you." Scarlet didn't say anything, she just clung to him, breathing in his precious scent.

She wouldn't be here when he came back.

* * * *

The wedding went off without a bobble. Annalise was radiant. Ethan strutted like a peacock and everyone else was duly attentive and appreciative. Scarlet sang beautifully, but Alex expected her to meet his eyes as she sang *Love Me Tender*, but she seldom looked up, and when she did, she looked over the heads of the audience. Alex held his breath as Scarlet walked down the aisle, déjà vu of exhilaration almost overwhelming him. But, as before, Scarlet never met his eyes. The toasts were said, the cakes were cut and no one could have asked for a more perfect wedding.

The bouquet was thrown and Scarlet managed to be somewhere else. There was going to be a delay in Annalise and Ethan's departure. Their flight to Hawaii had been delayed, so the sendoff wasn't quite what it would have been otherwise. The guests departed and the newlyweds retired to their room for some much needed downtime. Scarlet and Alex were preoccupied with trying to see all the hired help off and tying up loose ends. It would take at least a couple of hours to put everything back to some semblance of normal.

* * * *

When Alex wasn't looking, Scarlet crept up to the main house. She wanted to spend just a few minutes with Annalise and in her own way, tell her goodbye. Right now, she felt like she would be going home, but she had to think, she had to give Alex the benefit of the doubt. Maybe, if she just went away for a few hours, she could get her head on straight.

Best laid plans. When Scarlet reached Annalise's bedroom door, she heard the unmistakable sounds of two people making love. She should have known. "Oh, well."

Hearing the front door open, she tensed. "Scarlet!" It was Alex. "I'm going to the police station sweetie. I'll be back as soon as I can."

"Okay." She walked toward his voice, but before she could get there, he was gone.

* * * *

"When will I see you again?" Bobby held Cecile in his arms, his chin resting on her head. She was already packed and ready to head back to Dallas.

"It's not that far to Dallas, Bobby. We'll see each other." Doubts had blossomed in her heart, almost overnight. There was no way this was going to work. What had she been thinking?

"When?" He was determined to tie down specifics. "How about next weekend?"

Cecile refused to meet his direct gaze. "Give me a

call later in the week and I'll let you know."

"Are you giving me the brush-off, Ms. Fairchild?" Bobby's tone was light, but the words were clipped.

"Bobby...it's time for me to go." He loosened his embrace and let her back up a couple of feet.

"Fine." His voice was flat. "I'm not going to beg. You go back to Dallas. See your friends. But when you turn out the light at night and lay down in your bed, remember what it felt like when I pushed deep inside you. Remember what it felt like when I made you come apart in my arms." Bobby jerked her suitcase up and strode off to her car. "If you want to get away from me that bad, I'll help you."

Tears clamored in Cecile's throat. She would have no trouble remembering how it felt to love Bobby. No trouble at all.

* * * *

Alex met Officer Daisetta at the precinct building. "Come on in, Mr. Stewart, we've been expecting you." Alex followed the uniformed man into the cold, clinical rectangular room, turning down the offered coffee.

"There are some things that I think you need to hear." Officer Daisetta pointed to a chair, which Alex took. "It's not often that a criminal offers us irrefutable evidence, but this man is a piece of work."

"That he is." The officer took out LeBeau's digital recorder and set it to play. Every word that Rick and Scarlet had said was played for Alex to hear. He heard Rick's description of the physical pain he inflicted, he heard the lies he told Scarlet about his love and their marriage. Ice cold panic flowed through Alex's veins that once ran warm with life giving blood. This explained Scarlet's behavior. This explained why she wouldn't meet his eyes. This explained— "Oh, God.

Thanks, officer, but I've got to go."

* * * *

Scarlet didn't pack everything, and she took nothing that Alex had given her. She even went so far as to remove the diamond jewelry he had gifted to her, but in the end she kept the bracelet, after all, it was engraved. She left the insurance card, without a marriage, it was just a piece of plastic. And she left a note.

> *Dear Alex,*
>
> *I need to get away, to think. Just for a little while, I won't be gone too long. When I return, you can tell me what we need to do to straighten this out so nobody gets hurt. I can't pretend to understand what has happened. I am very torn about it all. I know Rick is a liar and I trust you. Beyond that, I am unbelievably confused. The only thing that keeps coming to my mind is the old saying, if it seems too good to be true, it probably is.*
>
> *Nevertheless, I do not regret a moment that I have spent with you. If it was all pretend, then I'm really no worse off than when I walked up the sidewalk with my bucket list. You've been wonderful, you've given me happiness that I never would have experienced otherwise.*
>
> *Speaking for myself – I love you,*
> *Scarlet.*

When Alex drove up in front of Lost Maples, he knew she was gone. The little car that had been parked over to one side for these many days was now absent. The lovely Bed and Breakfast had a forsaken look about it. Alex knew it was totally his imagination, the B&B was still clad in its wedding finery. Checking in the garage, he saw that Ethan and Annalise were still here, as was Bobby and Cecile. Everyone was here, except the person that mattered the most to him.

Taking the steps, two at a time, he tore into the front door. He wanted to scream, but first he had to make sure she had left no note, anything that would give him an inkling as to where she might be and what was going on. After hearing the tape that Rick had made, Alex knew exactly what Scarlet was thinking. It nearly killed him to imagine that Scarlet was under the impression he had betrayed her.

Racing to his room, he found the note on his pillow.

Reading the words was bad enough, but seeing the tear stains broke his heart.

* * * *

Scarlet had forgotten she was broke. She had been living in such a fantasy world, that the reality of having to worry about day-to-day problems seemed foreign to her. Looping back toward the B&B, she decided to go back to the park where she had spent that first glorious night with Alex. There were picnic tables and rest room facilities, and she had spent the night in her car before. Stopping at a convenience store, she bought two bottles of water and some cheese crackers. Now she was officially broke. What she was going to do for gas to get home on would have to remain a mystery, at least until she could get her head on straight.

Parking in the shade, Scarlet rolled down the

window to enjoy the cool fall breeze. Then quickly rolled it up when she realized how cool it actually was. Scooting her car seat all the way back, she shut her eyes and let the events of the day wash over her. As soon as she was still, pain knifed through her like the point of a sword. She regretted the turmoil of her childhood and the misunderstandings that she had with her father. She missed Alex, or at least she missed what she thought they had together. Even today, he had been so sweet and so attentive. How could this all be a lie?

Fumbling in her purse, she found her cell phone. This would have to go back to Alex also, she couldn't afford to keep it. She hesitated to turn it on, if he called, she didn't know if she could talk to him. Not yet. And there was very little juice left in the battery. Without a charger, it wouldn't last much longer. But she turned it on, because he had asked her to keep it with her and to keep it on. Immediately, the cell phone went off. Picking it up, she checked the number. It wasn't Alex. It was the doctor. Crap!

"Hello?"

"Scarlet? This is Doc Gibbs."

"Yes, sir?" She had already talked to him once today. She knew she was getting worse. And there wasn't a damn thing she could do about it. What more could he say now?

"Scarlet, the cross match has come back. The transplant is a go. I need for you to come in first thing in the morning. You, my dear girl, are about to get yourself a brand new kidney and a new lease on life."

"What? I don't understand. I'm not getting a transplant. Are you sure you called the right person?" This was cruel.

"I know who I'm talking to. Your husband is an approved donor. He passed the tests with flying colors." Emotion slammed into Scarlet's chest like a wrecker ball.

"Alex wants to give me a kidney?"

"He's already paid for the transplant. Insurance wouldn't cover it, he sat down in front of me and wrote out a check to pay for the entire thing. That man worships the ground you walk on."

Scarlet almost lost consciousness. Alex did love her. There was no other explanation. One did not fork out $375,000 on a joke. "I'll have to get back to you, doctor. I need to talk to my husband, first. Have you called him?"

"He's not answering his phone. I presumed that you two were together."

"We soon will be. We soon will be." She capped up her water and turned the key in the engine. It was time to go home.

* * * *

"Shit! Shit! Shit!" Alex wanted to punch a hole in the wall. He didn't have a clue where to look for her. He had tried her cell phone a dozen times, but she had it turned off. For the last hour or so, he had driven to the nearby towns and checked every hotel and motel. Nothing. Where in the hell could she be? She was sick. She was sad and she was lonely. And by God, she was his. And if he didn't find her soon, he would lose his mind.

"Ethan! Ethan!" He knew that the love birds were getting a head start on their honeymoon, but damn it, this was an emergency!! "Bobby! Bobby!" Alex was bringing down the roof.

* * * *

Chaos reigned supreme at the county jail. Rick

LeBeau didn't look dangerous, but madness brings with it a surprising strength. One moment of inattention and LeBeau had taken the guard's gun. He let out a loud yell and started shooting. Before he was through there was one dead and three wounded. And he was gone.

* * * *

Scarlet started back toward the B&B. This time, she would tell Alex what she was thinking and listen to his explanation. She was ashamed that she had forgotten one undeniable truth. She could trust Alex. He wouldn't lie to her. He loved her. She believed that with all of her heart. Nobody would ever convince her otherwise again.

But taking his kidney?

That was another matter altogether.

But that he wanted to give it her, had paid for the transplant. That was more than enough proof for Scarlet that she was loved. She was loved above all others.

Breaking every speed record known to man, Scarlet headed home.

* * * *

Alex threw his cell phone against the wall. If he couldn't call Scarlet with it, it was a useless piece of crap. The phone in the office rang and Alex sprinted for it, hoping against hope that it was his sweetheart. He never made it to the phone. From out of nowhere, a cold piece of steel stopped him in his tracks. The end of a gun barrel was being held securely to his right temple. "I've killed one man today, Stewart. It wouldn't bother me a bit to make it two."

"You piece of shit! You don't know what your lies have done." The word fear wasn't even in Alex's vocabulary—not for himself. The only reason he hesitated at all was because he wanted to live to make things right with Scarlet.

"I know exactly what I've done. And I've come to finish the job. Where is she?" He pushed the gun into Alex's skull. Alex never flinched.

"She's not here, you idiot. And if she was, do you really think I'd let you have her?" Alex glanced around, looking for anything that he could use to bash this monster's head in.

"Look, I'll get out of your life. I can live without your crappy job. But I want the church mouse. I want my sister. We've got a lot of time to make up for. If you'll turn her over to me, I'll let you live." Alex's blood ran cold. This man was truly crazy. And he wanted Scarlet. There wasn't a doubt in Alex's mind that Rick would kill Scarlet at the first opportunity.

"Over my dead body, LeBeau." Alex's words were said with the truest conviction that Scarlet had ever heard.

Scarlet had slipped in the front door, anxious to find her husband. Words of apology were on her lips, she never should have doubted him. He had never given her any reason to doubt, it had all been lies—lies perpetuated by a conniving maniac. Before she could call out his name, she heard a familiar voice. Rick LeBeau. Easing down the hall, she walked into the office area and saw a sight that made her blood run cold. LeBeau held a gun to Alex's head and from what he was saying, she was the only one that could save him.

"I'm here, Rick. You can let him go." At that moment, everything fell into place for Scarlet. She understood why Alex would be willing to give her his kidney. She understood why her friends' brother had never given a second thought to saving his sister's life. Scarlet understood how much she was loved, for she loved him just as deeply. "I'll gladly take his place. I love him. Just let him go."

"No, Scarlet." Alex sounded like he was in anguish. "No."

Scarlet tensed, every cell of her body was primed and ready to take Alex's place.

"Easy, Scarlet. I'm right behind you." Ethan's whispered voice was the most welcome sound she had ever heard. "Wait until I tell you, then walk forward, slowly. Bobby is going to come up behind LeBeau and when he turns Alex loose, our football player will take him out before he even knows what hit him. Are you with me?"

"Absolutely," she deadpanned.

* * * *

"Please, Scarlet. Baby, just turn around and walk away. I'll deal with this maniac." Alex was at the end of his rope. To his horror, she began to move forward. He watched her sweet eyes as they locked onto his. Alex was prepared to elbow backwards into LeBeau's body as hard as he could and then try and twist around to wrench the gun from his grasp. He had to do something before the bastard got his hands on Scarlet.

Before, he could do anything there was a blur of activity. Rick grabbed for Scarlet. Alex reacted, but his brothers came out of nowhere. Bobby flew through the air and landed squarely on top of the smaller man. Ethan grabbed the gun and Alex grabbed Scarlet. "Don't you *ever, ever, ever* put yourself in danger like that again." He wasn't shouting, he was talking so low that only she could hear. He wasn't holding her harshly, or roughly, he was holding her like she was made of spun glass.

Fitting herself to him, she answered. "How? Like you're ready to put yourself in danger to give me a kidney?" Realizing that she was back in his arms, he relaxed and just held her, searching for the words to say that he knew she needed to hear.

"So, you heard about that did you?" His lips weren't still. He kissed her eyes, her cheeks, her throat, assuring himself that she was whole and unharmed.

"Yeah, I got a phone call from the doctor just a few minutes ago. I was coming to talk to you about it. When I walked in and saw that monster was holding a gun to your head, I nearly went crazy. There is nothing in this world that I wouldn't do for you."

"I know. I have it in writing, in my pocket, and I'm holding you to it." His eyes locked with hers, he was not accepting no for an answer. "I want to hear you say yes to several questions I have to ask. Let me tell you the questions and you can practice saying yes. Scarlet, do you love me? Scarlet, will you love me forever? Scarlet, will you allow me to save your life? Please?"

At his whispered pleas, she smiled. "Maybe we can compromise. Maybe we can work something out. I'll admit that seeing you in danger with LeBeau's gun to your head and realizing that I could save you, I understand better now how you feel about the transplant."

"Good, because I was desperate to convince you that my giving you a kidney was the perfect answer to all of our problems."

"But, you had to pay cash for it, and it is so expensive. Even if we were married, insurance wouldn't cover it."

A flurry of activity forced Alex to pull Scarlet out of the hall and into his bedroom. The police had arrived and were talking to Bobby and Ethan as they took the handcuffed LeBeau back into custody. "I will straighten out the confusion over the license as soon as possible. If we have to redo the ceremony, we will. But Scarlet, you have to know nothing that Rick said about me was true."

Alex sat down on his bed and settled her on his lap. "He had this irritating habit of recording every conversation that he had with anybody. Those words that you heard me say were electronically manipulated, I didn't say those things."

Laying her head on his chest, she sighed. "I know. I have to admit that for a little while I didn't know what to think. And when the woman at the county clerk's office called and told me we weren't really married, it all began to make horrible sense."

"The woman was Sandy Moffett. I don't know how they managed to team up, that's still a mystery, but she and LeBeau conspired to try and mess things up for us. Sandy has it in for me about as much as LeBeau has it in for you." He pushed her collar aside and kissed the dark marks that marred the soft skin of her neck. "I am so sorry that you had to go through this. All I wanted to do was keep you safe and make you happy."

"The transplant is costing you so much money." Laying her forehead on his, she rubbed her palms up and down the muscles of his shoulders.

"Scarlet, you know that I love my Newmar Essex, don't you?" She met his eyes, obviously trying to figure out what he was getting at.

"Yes, I do. It's a beautiful RV."

"Would you agree that I love you more than I love that RV?"

"Yes. I know that you love me more."

"I paid six hundred thousand dollars for that mobile home. How much more do you think I would pay to save your life? There wasn't even a question about it. I would give everything I own for a chance to have an extra day with you, much less a lifetime." She threw her arms around him and held him close.

Scarlet Rose was going to live.

* * * *

When Alex woke up from the surgery, his first thought was of his wife. "Ethan?"

Ethan and Annalise had postponed their honeymoon. Staying with his brother and her sister while they went through major surgery was much more important. Annalise had been flabbergasted to find out that Scarlet had lived all those years with the threat of death hanging over her head.

"I'm here, buddy."

"Scarlet?"

"She came through with flying colors. Annalise is with her."

"I want to go to her."

"Not yet, it'll be a few days before they let you get out of this bed."

"Roll me in there. Roll the whole damn bed."

"Do you want to get us into all sorts of trouble?"

"Ethan, take me to Scarlet. Now."

"Bobby, I'm going to need some help here." It was a sight to behold. The oldest and the youngest Stewarts rolling a hospital bed down the corridor that contained their bigger, totally determined brother.

"Good grief." Annalise laughed when she opened the door to the private room that her sister occupied.

"They might as well make room in here for him, he's not going to put up with being away from her even for a minute." Ethan huffed as he maneuvered the hospital bed through the door. Bobby worked, shifting Scarlet's bed and her monitoring equipment over to allow the additional bed to be placed side by side.

"Be careful with her," Alex cautioned. No one argued with him. They just did as he said. "Is she awake?"

"No," Annalise went over and took her brother in

law's hand. "She woke up for just a few seconds a while ago, but she dropped right back off. Alex, I want to thank you. For everything. For saving my sister's life and for loving her enough to do it."

"I adore her, Annalise. I would die for her, daily. This was no hardship at all. Did she say anything?" Alex strained to see Scarlet's face.

"Your name, and she asked how you were."

"That's my baby. Move the beds closer together. I want to hold her hand." They pushed and pulled until the beds were close enough that Alex could reach over and clasp Scarlet's hand. When he did, she opened her eyes.

"Alex?"

"I'm here, love. How do you feel?"

"Perfect."

"Do you need anything?"

"You."

"You've got me love, for the rest of your life, you've got me."

Chapter Nine Epilogue

When Alex pulled the RV into the camping area at Graceland, he looked over at the sparkling eyes of his beloved wife. "We're here, baby. Memphis, Tennessee. Home of the King of Rock and Roll."

"Thank you, Alex. I know this isn't most men's idea of a honeymoon destination."

"Sweetheart, as long as I have you, and that King Size bed in the back, I don't care where we go."

Philip Alexander Stewart had a terminal case of Scarlet Fever and he had no intention of looking for a cure.

Sign up for Sable's Newsletter
http://eepurl.com/qRvyn

Now for a glimpse into Book 3 –

Bobby Does Dallas

Hill Country Heart

"I've missed you, Bobby."

"Missing you is a mild way to put it. I haven't breathed since we've been apart." He walked up to her slowly. His manhood got to her a couple of seconds before the rest of him did; she had never seen him so fully engorged. With a soft touch, she caressed the hard shaft, marveling that in a few moments it would be wholly contained within the aching depths of her body.

He lifted up her hair, cupping his hands behind her neck and captured her mouth in a deep, searing kiss that had her clit peeking out of its hood and begging for attention. "Hmmmm, Baby. Your lips are so sweet." With hungry hands he soothed all over her body, from shoulder to hand, from neck to the cleavage that seemed to fascinate him so. In a move she wasn't expecting, he knelt at her feet and ran his hands up under her gown, caressing her legs from ankles to hip. "I've dreamed about touching you for months, Ceelee. It's been almost a year!" He laughed. "Jaidon's proof of that, a year since I touched you, a year since I sucked your nipples, a year since I pushed my cock into the haven of your body." He pressed his forehead into her abdomen and just inhaled her scent. "God, I want all of you. I'm overwhelmed. I've got to slow down. If I don't, I'm gonna explode just from touching your skin."

Cecile held out her hand. "Come with me. We've got all night. Let me give you some relief." She guided him to sit on the bed and lean back against the headboard. He watched with fire in his eyes as she skimmed the gown over her head leaving her nude. "I've never done this before, but I bet I can figure it out." Joining him on the bed, she backed up to him, straddling his legs and spreading her thighs, giving him full access to her womanhood. "Guide him in; I'm more than ready for you."

"I'm being selfish. I've done nothing to ready you or prepare you. But, hell, I've been celibate for almost nine months and my control is gone. I'll make it up to you, I promise."

As she sank down onto his iron-hard cock, the relief of his invasion was unspeakable. "Nothing to make up," she gasped. "I want this more than you do."

"Seriously doubting that." Bobby groaned at the tight, wet heaven that welcomed him. "Sinking into you is like being massaged by warm, whipped cream. Do you know what this position is called, Ceelee?" He held on to her hips while she proceeded to try and ride him into insanity.

"Wonderful?" She didn't have her full wits about her, all she wanted to do was grind her pussy down on his groin and whimper.

"It's a reverse cowgirl. Fittin' huh?" He pulled her back against his chest and angled her so he could drive her crazy with short hard jabs.

"It fits just fine," she let her head rest on his shoulder. "Touch my breasts, please?" She was beyond being embarrassed about begging; her whole body was about to go up in flames.

"Oh, yeah!" he breathed into her ear. "Two handfuls of delight." He lifted and molded them, massaging the pink areolas and pulling on the nipples.

Darts of ecstasy shot through her at his welcome attention to her breasts. But when milk started coating his fingers, she stiffened—not knowing how he was going to react. "Sorry," she whispered.

Bobby bit her on the neck and ground his cock up harder and deeper. "That's the sexiest damn thing I've ever seen." He licked the milk off of his fingers. "If that didn't belong to my baby boy, I'd give my eyeteeth to have a taste."

"There's plenty for both of you." She wanted to say more to him, she really did, but it felt so good. When he moved one hand down to rub on her clit she lost it, just flat lost it. "Bobby!" she screamed as her world exploded. He held her tight as she quaked and jerked in his arms.

"Lord, I missed this. Your little pussy is hugging my cock and fluttering around me, Sweet Jesus, Baby, you are unbelievable!" Bobby didn't let up in his piston-like movements. With constant touches, he rubbed her body, fondled her breasts and led her from satisfaction back to full arousal. "I can't get enough of you."

Cecile laughed. "Don't get me wrong. I love it. But, you've never talked this much when we made love."

Bobby laughed too. And his answer brought tears to her eyes. "I can't help it, Ceelee. I'm just so happy to be here. I can't hush." With one strong movement of his body, he propelled them down in the bed so that they were lying flat. She was still impaled on his cock, but now she was lying back on his body, fully supine. "Hold on, Honey. This is my grand finale." He lifted his legs so his knees were bent, giving him greater ability to move his hips. Grasping her breasts, he bucked his hips and carried her on a ride to the stars. "I love you. I love you. I love you," he chanted in her ear as their orgasms crashed in a simultaneous wave of rapture.

They cuddled and they whispered, but soon they lay still just enjoying holding one another again. Cecile lay on her side. She rubbed his chest in a movement of contemplation and contentment. His eyes were still closed and his breathing was just now settling down to something near normal. She wanted to ask him what the future held for them, but she bit her tongue. That would come, or it wouldn't. Placing one kiss in the center of his chest, she vowed not to pressure him. He talked like he wanted to be a part of her and Jaidon's life, but Bobby was young, handsome and had the world by the tail. It wouldn't be fair of her to make any demands.

To her right, the baby monitor let her know that somebody wasn't happy. "I bet he's wet. I'll be right back." She slipped from the bed, grabbed her robe, and headed to the nursery. Footsteps falling behind her let her know that Bobby was right behind her.

"Let me do it. I need to learn." He had hastily pulled on his pants, determined not to be left out. She helped him gather everything he needed and showed him how to lower the side of the crib so he could change his first diaper.

It was so sweet, Jaidon was so small and Bobby was so big. His hands dwarfed the baby's legs and Jaidon was in a kicking, squirming mood. "I'm gonna hog-tie you, Boy," Bobby started playing with his son. "I've wrestled steers to the ground. I think I can handle a tiny mite like you."

Cecile wasn't so sure. When he took the diaper off and was met with a fountain of little-boy wee-wee spurting up at him, she thought she would die laughing.

"What in tarnation!" Bobby covered the erupting geyser with the diaper and looked at Cecile in horror. "Did you know they would do that?"

She couldn't answer for laughing. Every time he moved the diaper, Jaidon let loose with another spurt. If he wasn't so young, she would have thought that he was playing a joke on his pop. "Yes. When he takes a notion to go, you have to cover him up and get out of the way."

Bobby stood to one side and lifted the corner of the diaper warily. "You little bugger, you." He got rid of the dirty diaper in the pail and then set out to clean and change him. She had to help with the diaper alignment, but Bobby caught on quickly. And when he bent over and began blowing raspberries on Jaidon's stomach, Cecile lost her heart forever. She was so happy she could burst. It felt like nothing could come between them or take away this joy.

She was wrong.

myBook.to/BobbyDoesDallas

COME WITH ME
Dixie Dreaming

Jake is the manager of the golf course at the country club. He's designing and overseeing a building project and the sight of him shirtless and sweating and flexing…has given Lacy ideas. Jake has a certain reputation of being able to handle almost any task he's given. Rumors of his sexual prowess are legendary. Now, every time Lacy sees him working with his hands, doing some heavy lifting, his body gleaming with the sheen of exertion – she begins to hope that Jake can give her what no one else ever has.

IF - she can just figure out how to ask him. But what Lacy doesn't know is that Jake has ideas of his own. His outlook on love and life has been molded by the mistakes of his family. He doesn't think true love exists, there's just sex. Until he meets Lacy. This Fourth of July celebration proves to have more explosions in store than those in the sky, for Jake sets out to prove that he can give Lacy exactly what she needs. In fact, Jake intends to show Lacy that what she needs – is him.

The Key to Micah's Heart
The HELL YEAH! Series

Micah Wolfe is one cocky, sexy, son-of-a-gun. He wears many hats–former intelligence officer, Equalizer, rancher, and a secret career that's about to become public knowledge–erotic writer Don Juan. To most he seems like an open book: flirtatious, audacious, and devil-may-care. But there's a side of Micah that he keeps locked away. He's been hurt, suffered loss, closed away parts of his heart so no one will have the power to hurt him again. But the winds of change are blowing…

Madison Fellows is at the end of her rope. For every step forward she gains, life knocks her back two. She can't even stay in her own apartment because she doesn't feel safe from her flighty mother's abusive husband. But sometimes the storms in life push us to the perfect place at the perfect time–Cinderella meets the man of her dreams when she least expects him. Madison runs to a homeless shelter where Micah is volunteering. Seeing her struggle to protect what little she has, he loans her a simple item that will become an unlikely symbol of their love. A lock. An ordinary lock.

Micah has no shortage of beautiful women; he attracts them like flowers draw bees. But there's something different about Madison–she's real, she's sweet and he fast becomes addicted to her taste. Join them on their journey of love fraught with adventure, intrigue and steamy to-die-for sex. The quintessential bachelor meets the woman he can't forget–the woman who'll hold The Key To Micah's Heart.

Texas C.H.A.O.S.
Texas Heroes Series

The letters C. H. A. O. S. don't just refer to reality out of control, it's an alert–the Chief Has Arrived On Scene! Logan Gray is that chief. He covers the ground he stands on and people show respect when he walks by. In his late thirties, Logan is a confirmed bachelor. While he may adore the young Jenna from afar, at 18, he considers her to be a lifetime too young for him.

Jenna is of another opinion. Logan Gray is everything to her. He rescued her from a fire at 16. His parents took her in when she had nothing and no one. Raised on his Gray Wolf guest ranch, Jenna learns how to trick-ride and perform in the rodeo. When Logan's not looking, she even loves to try her hand at bull-riding. And now, she is ready to go after what she wants most–Logan Gray.

Ignoring the fact that his heart and body craves Jenna like a drug, Logan does what he thinks is best and gently turns her down. What happens next turns his world on end. Logan learns that love can't be defined by a number and life without Jenna is no life at all.

T-R-O-U-B-L-E

Texas Heart Series

Trouble comes calling on Kyler Landon. He falls hard and fast for his beautiful, mysterious neighbor after she saves him from a rattlesnake attack. The sexual tension mounts between them with each sensual encounter, but he soon realizes that Cooper has been hurt and is leery of men. So he sets out to teach her that a real man can be gentle, loving, and sexy as hell.

Trouble seems to follow Cooper, and Ky makes it his mission to protect her from her past. Kyler would move heaven and earth to keep her in his bed and in his life.

Love's Magic Spell

Tory has one magical night to learn what love is all about.

Night after lonely night, she tosses in her solitary bed, longing to touch and be touched, to experience desire and rapture. Her body aches to know fulfillment, to be taken and possessed by a man—but only one man will do.

Raylan West is the man of her dreams, and Tory Summers would give everything she owns for a chance with him. But it isn't going to happen—a man like him is not for her. Unless…Tory finds a way.

Deep in the bayous of South Louisiana there are secrets, magical secrets. Hoodoo. Witchcraft. Will-o'-the-wisp floating over dark waters, lit by unearthly light.

Desperate for a chance, Tory places her faith in the supernatural. She travels deep into the swamp to acquire a love potion promised to bring Raylan under her spell for one night, one perfect moonlit Halloween night where anything is possible. For a few precious hours, Tory will be beautiful, desirable, and sexy in Raylan's eyes.

The only problem is…Tory wants the magic to last forever.

MURDER, MAGIC, VOODOO, WITCHCRAFT, LOTS OF LOUISIANA ATMOSPHERE

And plenty of STEAMY, SENSUAL, SEXY LOVE!!

A Breath of Heaven
The El Camino Real Series

Cade and Abby have a history. Years ago they were in love. Undeclared and unrequited, Cade waited until Abby was old enough for him to declare his love. Abby wanted nothing more than she wanted Cade.

But something happened.

Abby pushed Cade away and he never knew why. Since then, sparks fly when they're together. Antagonizing one another has become their favorite sport. The only problem is… it's all a front. They bicker because they both want the same thing – each other. A wedding brings them together and Cade is determined to learn Abby's secret. He'll do whatever it takes to win her love.

Meet the King Family of El Camino Real – five brothers, one sister and a legacy as big as Texas.

Rogue
The Son's of Dusty Walker

A loner by choice and a renegade by nature.

Rogue is living up to his name. He's lived life on his own terms, doing everything from team-roping in college, Texas Hold 'em champion to founding his own company, Lone Wolf Oil.

Everything he's accomplished has been in spite of Dusty Walker, a man who sired four sons by four women – none of them his wife. Rogue might be following in his father's footsteps, but he is nothing like his father.

And he never will be if he can help it.

When he flies to Kansas for the reading of Dusty's will, three brothers and a quarter interest in a half-billion dollar business aren't all he finds...Rogue feels like he's been hit by a tornado after he walks into a room and finds a woman in his bed. Not just any woman, either...

The last time he saw Kit Ross, she was racing off in her truck leaving him naked and hard by the side of the road. Of course, he deserved it; he'd hurt her. To say she wasn't happy to see him was an understatement. And when he wins her ranch with a good poker hand, the game is on.

It's not just poker that's being played. They can't keep their hands off one another. Rogue doesn't know if he has room in his life for family and love. He doesn't know if he can be trusted with people's hearts and happiness. What if he's more like Dusty Walker than he ever knew?

The Sons of Dusty Walker. Four brothers – one tainted legacy and a wild, wild ride.

Sweet Evangeline
Moon Magic Series

Evangeline is magical. She longs to find her soulmate - and being a woman of power - she whips up a spell and conjures him up.

Austin Firefighter Eric McCallister is enchanted by the beautiful woman who sculpted his likeness from a dream. Immediately, their attraction and chemistry burns like a wildfire.

But, all is not a fairy-tale. An arsonist is stalking Eric and someone is trying to kill Evangeline. On top of that, there's magick afoot that can call down storms, bring the dead back to life and break ancient curses. But, the greatest magick of all is the love Eric has for Sweet Evangeline.

If I Can Dream
The HELL YEAH! Series

The moment Tennessee McCoy lays eyes on Molly Reyes sitting astride a horse in the desert sun, love hits him like a bolt of lightning from out of the blue. She is his soulmate, his other half. They speak the same language, they want the same things. Their attraction is complete, the passion they share nearly consumes them. Knowing she is meant to be his, Ten can't wait to make her his bride. The future seems bright until happiness slips through their fingers like grains of sand.

When all seems hopeless, sometimes all we have left is our dreams. Ten can only believe what his eyes can see, what his ears can hear. Molly can't seem to find the words to make him understand that she would rather lose her soul than betray him. Now both Tennessee and Molly must learn to place their faith in one another, to hold fast to love and trust their hearts.

Their journey back to love will be one you'll never forget.

About the Author

Sable Hunter is a New York Times, USA Today bestselling author of nearly 50 books in 7 series. She writes sexy contemporary stories full of emotion and suspense. Her focus is mainly cowboy and novels set in Louisiana with a hint of the supernatural. Sable writes what she likes to read and enjoys putting her fantasies on paper. Her books are emotional tales where the heroine is faced with challenges. Her aim is to write a story that will make you laugh, cry and swoon. If she can wring those emotions from a reader, she has done her job. Sable resides in Austin, Texas with her two dogs. Passionate about all animals, she has been known to charm creatures from a one ton bull to a family of raccoons. For fun, Sable haunts cemeteries and battlefields armed with night-vision cameras and digital recorders hunting proof that love survives beyond the grave. Welcome to her world of magic, alpha heroes, sexy cowboys and hot, steamy to-die-for sex. Step into the shoes of her heroines and escape to places where right prevails, love conquers all and holding out for a hero is not an impossible dream

Visit Sable:

Website:

http://www.sablehunter.com

Facebook:

https://www.facebook.com/authorsablehunter

Amazon:

http://www.amazon.com/author/sablehunter

Pinterest

https://www.pinterest.com/AuthorSableH/

Twitter

https://twitter.com/huntersable

Bookbub:

https://www.bookbub.com/authors/sable-hunter

Goodreads:

https://www.goodreads.com/author/show/4419823.Sable_Hunter

Sign up for Sable Hunter's newsletter

http://eepurl.com/qRvyn

SABLE'S BOOKS
Get hot and bothered!!!

Hell Yeah!

Cowboy Heat

Hot on Her Trail

Her Magic Touch

Brown Eyed Handsome Man

Badass

Burning Love

Forget Me Never
With Ryan O'Leary & Jess Hunter

I'll See You In My Dreams
With Ryan O'Leary

Finding Dandi

Skye Blue

I'll Remember You

True Love's Fire

Thunderbird
With Ryan O'Leary

Welcome To My World

How to Rope a McCoy

One Man's Treasure
With Ryan O'Leary

You Are Always on My Mind

If I Can Dream

Head over Spurs

The Key to Micah's Heart
With Ryan O'Leary

Love Me, I Dare you!

Godsend (Hell Yeah! Heritage)

Because I Said So
(Crossover HELL YEAH!/Texas Heroes)

Hell Yeah! Sweeter Versions

Cowboy Heat

Hot on Her Trail

Her Magic Touch

Brown Eyed Handsome Man

Badass

Burning Love

Finding Dandi

Forget Me Never

I'll See You In My Dreams

Moon Magic Series
A Wishing Moon

Sweet Evangeline

Hill Country Heart Series
Unchained Melody

Scarlet Fever

Bobby Does Dallas

Dixie Dreaming
Come With Me

Pretty Face: A Red Hot Cajun Nights Story

Texas Heat Series
T-R-O-U-B-L-E

My Aliyah

El Camino Real Series
A Breath of Heaven

Loving Justice

Texas Heroes Series
Texas Wildfire

Texas CHAOS

Texas Lonestar

Texas Maverick

Because I Said So
(Crossover HELL YEAH!/Texas Heroes)

Other Titles from Sable Hunter:

For A Hero

Green With Envy (It's Just Sex Book 1)
with Ryan O'Leary

Hell Yeah! Box Set With Bonus Cookbook

Love's Magic Spell: A Red Hot Treats Story

Wolf Call

Cowboy 12 Pack: Twelve-Novel Boxed Set

Rogue (The Sons of Dusty Walker)

Kit and Rogue

Be My Love Song

Audio
Cowboy Heat - Sweeter Version: Hell Yeah! Sweeter Version

Hot on Her Trail - Sweeter Version: Hell Yeah! Sweeter Version, Book 2

Spanish Edition
Vaquero Ardiente *(*Cowboy Heat)

Su Rastro Caliente (Hot On Her Trail)

Printed in Great Britain
by Amazon